全民英檢

聽力通

三民英語編輯小組　彙編

三民書局

© 　全民英檢聽力通

彙　　　編	三民英語編輯小組
責任編輯	林宛瑜
美術設計	黃顯喬
插畫設計	許天虹

發 行 人	劉振強
著作財產權人	三民書局股份有限公司
發 行 所	三民書局股份有限公司
	地址　臺北市復興北路386號
	電話　(02)25006600
	郵撥帳號　0009998-5
門 市 部	(復北店)臺北市復興北路386號
	(重南店)臺北市重慶南路一段61號

| 出版日期 | 初版一刷　中華民國九十八年六月 |
| 編　　　號 | S 808090 |

行政院新聞局登記證局版臺業字第○二○○號

有著作權‧不准侵害

ISBN　978-957-14-5187-9　　（平裝）

http://www.sanmin.com.tw　三民網路書店

※本書如有缺頁、破損或裝訂錯誤，請寄回本公司更換。

給讀者的話

本書採用口袋型設計，搭配聽力測驗 MP3 光碟，主要是提供給需要熟悉全民英檢中級考試，且希望能隨時隨地增強實力的讀者。除此之外，對於有意提昇英語聽力的人而言，也是一大隨身利器。

本書共有 6 回模擬試題，每回涵蓋的題型——看圖辨義、問答、簡短對話，測驗內容、題數以及難度完全比照全民英檢聽力測驗的出題形式與方向。每回試題後即附上聽力腳本、翻譯與解析，以利讀者迅速掌握重點、修正錯誤。本書之錄音內容由專業外籍錄音員錄製，且力求完全模擬實際測驗之題目間隔與速度。

藉由本書，讀者能有效提升應試熟悉度並增加實戰經驗。希望本書能幫助想要通過全民英檢中級考試的讀者，面對聽力測驗時得心應手，順利過關。

三民英語編輯小組　謹誌

CONTENTS

此部分有 15 題，每題都有一張與該題目相對應的圖畫。請聽錄音機播出題目以及 A、B、C、D 四個英語敘述之後，選出與所看到的圖畫最相符的答案。每題只播出一遍。

1

Kent County Library

Opening Hours

Tuesday to Friday

08 : 00 - 21 : 00

Saturday and Sunday

09 : 00 - 17 : 00

2

3

4

5

6

7

8

9

10

11

12

13

14

15

Track #02

此部分有 15 題，每題請聽錄音機播出一個英語句子之後，從 A、B、C、D 四個回答或回應中，選出一個最適合者作答。每題只播出一遍。

___ 16 (A) I'm glad to hear that.
　　(B) Everything will be fine.
　　(C) My dog died this morning.
　　(D) You have the wrong number.

___ 17 (A) Yes. I'd like to make a room reservation.
　　(B) Yes. It'll be $450 per person.
　　(C) Yes. I just saw a hit-and-run accident.
　　(D) Yes. I'll tell her that you called.

___ 18 (A) Sure. The gallery is on the second floor.
　　(B) OK. I'll take care of it for you.
　　(C) Sorry, we don't take credit cards.
　　(D) Sorry. You have to leave it at the counter.

19 (A) Yeah, I collect stamps.

(B) No, thanks. I still have some.

(C) Yes. By airmail, please.

(D) All right, here is your change.

20 (A) Yes. I'm a registered member.

(B) Sure, let me get it for you.

(C) No. It'll take three days.

(D) No. Just regular, please.

21 (A) Sure. It'll be no trouble at all.

(B) Yes. Just a couple of CDs.

(C) By express mail, please.

(D) OK. Here you are.

22 (A) Separate bills, please.

(B) Here is your tip.

(C) Yes. It's 10%.

(D) No, thanks.

23 (A) I'd like to leave a message.

(B) Please dial "0" for emergency.

(C) First dial "9" and then dial the number.

(D) You can dial "2" for room service.

24 (A) Yes. It's right down the hall.

    (B) Sure. I'll send it to your room right away.

    (C) I'm afraid you can't pay by credit card there.

    (D) I'm sorry. The newspapers are sold out.

25 (A) Sure. Wait a moment, please.

    (B) Yes. You can find it in our store.

    (C) Sorry. It'll be sent up right away.

    (D) Please dial "9" for outside calls.

26 (A) Monday to Friday.

    (B) 7:00 a.m. to 9:00 p.m.

    (C) It's 2:30 p.m. now.

    (D) 5:00 in the morning.

27 (A) No. It runs every half hour.

    (B) Yes. It stops at all major hotels.

    (C) Sure. Are you checking in now?

    (D) Yes. Where are you heading for?

28 (A) Please pay at that counter over there.

    (B) It'll take you about 40 minutes.

(C) You'll need your passport and credit card for renting a car.

(D) Go straight ahead and you'll see the car rental desk on your left.

___29 (A) Two double rooms, please.

(B) A trip to Hawaii sounds great.

(C) I'll stay in Spring Hotel. How about you?

(D) Six nights. Could you give me a discount?

___30 (A) Yes, there are two within walking distance.

(B) Yes. It's 90 US dollars per night.

(C) Sounds OK. You can get there by shuttle bus.

(D) All rooms on the non-smoking floors are full.

此部分有 15 題，每題請聽錄音機播出一段對話及一個相關的問題，然後從 A、B、C、D 四個選項中挑出一個最適合的答案。每題只播出一遍。

_____ 31 (A) The service counter.
　　　　 (B) Some change.
　　　　 (C) A copy machine.
　　　　 (D) Some magazine articles.

_____ 32 (A) He didn't buy a train ticket.
　　　　 (B) He didn't return the library book on time.
　　　　 (C) He didn't recycle his plastic bottles.
　　　　 (D) He parked his car in the non-parking zone.

_____ 33 (A) Science fiction.
　　　　 (B) Detective stories.
　　　　 (C) Historical novels.
　　　　 (D) Romantic novels.

_____ 34 (A) It is too small.

(B) Its color is not right.

(C) Its style is too old-fashioned.

(D) It is too expensive.

35 (A) His personal life.

(B) His job.

(C) His weight.

(D) His new restaurant.

36 (A) Library rules.

(B) Job interviews.

(C) Cafeterias in schools.

(D) Available jobs on campus.

37 (A) The Dance Club.

(B) The Art Club.

(C) The Drama Club.

(D) The Guitar Club.

38 (A) She is a chef.

(B) She is a graduate student.

(C) She is a teacher in a cooking school.

(D) She is a restaurant owner.

39 (A) A police officer.

(B) A doctor.

(C) A professor.

(D) A reporter.

40 (A) Tim has already been to Spain.

(B) Neither Tim nor Jenny can speak Spanish.

(C) Spain is too far to travel to.

(D) Other places are cheaper to visit.

41 (A) Australia has beautiful scenery.

(B) The man is going to Australia.

(C) The man has no plans for his New Year's vacation.

(D) The woman has no money to go to Australia.

42 (A) Ride the train.

(B) Enjoy the hot springs.

(C) See the forest.

(D) See the sunrise.

43 (A) Three. (B) Four.

(C) Five. (D) Six.

44 (A) June 20th. (B) July 30th.

(C) June 13th. (D) July 23rd.

45 (A) In the first class.

(B) In the business class.

(C) In the economy class.

(D) None of the above.

1. When is the library closed?

   (A) Monday.　　　　　　(B) Wednesday.

   (C) Thursday.　　　　　(D) Sunday.

   問題：這個圖書館何時休館？

   選項：(A) 星期一。　　　(B) 星期三。

   　　　(C) 星期四。　　　(D) 星期天。

---

2. How many books is the girl checking out?

   (A) One.　　　　　　　(B) Two.

   (C) Three.　　　　　　(D) Four.

   問題：這個女生要借出幾本書？

   選項：(A) 一本。　　　　(B) 兩本。

   　　　(C) 三本。　　　　(D) 四本。

   提示：check out 在此表示「借出」。

---

3. What does the picture tell you?

   (A) No smoking in the sickroom.

   (B) No cell phones in the sickroom.

   (C) No talking in the sickroom.

   (D) No food or drinks in the sickroom.

   問題：這張圖畫告訴你什麼？

選項：(A) 病房裡禁止吸煙。

(B) 病房裡禁用手機。

(C) 病房裡禁止交談。

(D) 病房裡禁止飲食。

---

4. What is happening?

(A) The boy is riding his bicycle.

(B) The boy is fixing his bicycle.

(C) The boy's bicycle is broken.

(D) The boy's bicycle is gone.

問題：發生什麼事？

選項：(A) 男孩正在騎他的腳踏車。

(B) 男孩正在修他的腳踏車。

(C) 男孩的腳踏車壞掉了。

(D) 男孩的腳踏車不見了。

---

5. What does the woman do?

(A) She is a singer.

(B) She is a waitress.

(C) She is a photographer.

(D) She is a babysitter.

問題：這個女子是做什麼的？

選項：(A) 她是歌手。　　(B) 她是女服務生。

(C) 她是攝影師。　　(D) 她是保姆。

6. What are the men doing?

   (A) Boarding a plane.

   (B) Getting their baggage.

   (C) Going through security.

   (D) Going through immigration.

   問題：這兩名男子在做什麼？

   選項：(A) 登機。

   　　　(B) 拿取他們的行李。

   　　　(C) 通過安檢。

   　　　(D) 接受入境審查。

   提示：security 在此指機場裡的安全檢查，所有旅客
   　　　登機前都必須通過的地方；immigration 則
   　　　是指入境前旅客必須接受入境審查。

---

7. What is the flight attendant doing?

   (A) Helping passengers find their seats.

   (B) Delivering meals to passengers.

   (C) Asking passengers to fasten their seat belts.

   (D) Demonstrating how to put on a life vest.

   問題：這位空服人員正在做什麼？

   選項：(A) 幫忙乘客找座位。

   　　　(B) 送餐點給乘客。

   　　　(C) 要求乘客繫上安全帶。

(D) 示範如何穿上救生衣。

---

8. What does the flight attendant want the passenger to do?

(A) Give her tray to him.

(B) Go back to her seat.

(C) Put her seat in the upright position.

(D) Turn off her cell phone.

問題：這位空服人員要乘客做什麼？

選項：(A) 將她的餐盤給他。

(B) 回到她的座位。

(C) 豎直她的椅背。

(D) 關掉她的手機。

---

9. Where are they?

(A) In a hotel. (B) In a clinic.

(C) At a restaurant. (D) On an airplane.

問題：他們在哪裡？

選項：(A) 在旅館裡。 (B) 在診所裡。

(C) 在餐廳裡。 (D) 在飛機上。

---

10. What happens to the boy?

(A) He has a fever.

(B) He has a stomachache.

(C) He has a headache.

(D) He has a toothache.

問題：這個男孩怎麼了？

選項：(A) 他發燒。　　　(B) 他胃痛。

(C) 他頭痛。　　　(D) 他牙痛。

---

11. What is the woman doing?

(A) Stopping the man from taking pictures.

(B) Stopping the man from smoking.

(C) Asking the man not to eat in the room.

(D) Asking the man not to touch the painting.

問題：這位女子在做什麼？

選項：(A) 阻止男子拍照。

(B) 阻止男子抽菸。

(C) 要求男子不要在室內吃東西。

(D) 要求男子不要觸碰畫作。

---

12. What did the customers NOT order?

(A) Coffee.　　　　　(B) Cheese cake.

(C) Chef's Salad.　　(D) Club Sandwich.

問題：客人們沒有點什麼？

選項：(A) 咖啡。　　　(B) 起司蛋糕。

(C) 主廚沙拉。　　(D) 總匯三明治。

13. What is happening?

(A) The waiter is taking the woman's order.

(B) The waiter is giving the woman the menu.

(C) The woman is paying her bill by credit card.

(D) The woman is complaining about the food.

問題：發生什麼事？

選項：(A) 服務員正在為女子點餐。

(B) 服務員正在給女子菜單。

(C) 女子正要以信用卡付帳。

(D) 女子正在抱怨食物。

14. What are the men doing?

(A) Fighting with each other.

(B) Sharing the cost of their meals.

(C) Asking the waitress to bring a menu.

(D) Paying their bill in cash.

問題：這兩位男子正在做什麼？

選項：(A) 和對方吵架。

(B) 分攤餐點的費用。

(C) 要女服務生拿菜單來。

(D) 以現金付帳。

15. How often does the train run from Boston to New York City?

(A) Once a day.　　　　(B) Once a week.

(C) Four times a day.　　(D) Four times a week.

問題：從波士頓到紐約市的火車發車頻率為何？

選項：(A) 一天一次。　　　(B) 一週一次。

　　　(C) 一天四次。　　　(D) 一週四次。

第二部分　腳本與解析

Track #02

16. You look very sad. What's wrong?

(A) I'm glad to hear that.

(B) Everything will be fine.

(C) My dog died this morning.

(D) You have the wrong number.

問題：你看起很難過，怎麼了嗎？

選項：(A) 我很高興聽到這消息。

　　　(B) 一切都會沒事的。

　　　(C) 我的狗今天早上死掉了。

　　　(D) 你打錯電話了。

17. Police station, may I help you?

(A) Yes. I'd like to make a room reservation.

(B) Yes. It'll be $450 per person.

(C) Yes. I just saw a hit-and-run accident.

(D) Yes. I'll tell her that you called.

問題：警察局，有什麼需要幫忙的嗎？

選項：(A) 是的，我想要訂房。

(B) 好的，每個人是 450 元。

(C) 是的，我剛看見一起肇事逃逸的車禍。

(D) 好的，我會告訴她你來過電話。

提示：hit-and-run 表示「撞了人就跑的」。

---

18. May I take my backpack into the gallery?

(A) Sure. The gallery is on the second floor.

(B) OK. I'll take care of it for you.

(C) Sorry, we don't take credit cards.

(D) Sorry. You have to leave it at the counter.

問題：我可以將我的背包帶進畫廊嗎？

選項：(A) 當然。書廊在二樓。

(B) 好的。我會幫你保管它。

(C) 抱歉，我們不收信用卡。

(D) 抱歉。你必須將它留在櫃檯。

---

19. Do you need to buy some stamps?

(A) Yeah, I collect stamps.

(B) No, thanks. I still have some.

(C) Yes. By airmail, please.

(D) All right, here is your change.

問題：你需要買些郵票嗎？

選項：(A) 是啊，我有收集郵票。

　　　(B) 不，謝了。我還有一些。

　　　(C) 是的，麻煩以航空郵寄。

　　　(D) 好了，這是你的找零。

提示：change 在此為名詞，表示「零錢」。

---

20. Do you want to send it by registered mail?

　　(A) Yes. I'm a registered member.

　　(B) Sure, let me get it for you.

　　(C) No. It'll take three days.

　　(D) No. Just regular, please.

問題：你要以掛號信寄出嗎？

選項：(A) 是，我是已註冊的會員。

　　　(B) 當然，讓我為你拿來。

　　　(C) 不，那將費時三天。

　　　(D) 不，麻煩一般就好。

提示：問題中的 registered mail 意思是「掛號信」，
　　　而在選項中的 registered 則表「已註冊登記
　　　的」。

---

21. Could you tell me what is inside the package?

　　(A) Sure. It'll be no trouble at all.

　　(B) Yes. Just a couple of CDs.

(C) By express mail, please.

(D) OK. Here you are.

問題：你可以告訴我包裹裡面是什麼嗎？

選項：(A) 當然，那一點都不麻煩。

　　　(B) 好的，只是幾張唱片。

　　　(C) 麻煩以快遞方式寄送。

　　　(D) 好的，拿去吧。

提示：by express mail 或 by express 都表示「以快遞方式寄送」。

---

22. Does the bill include a service charge?

(A) Separate bills, please.

(B) Here is your tip.

(C) Yes. It's 10%.

(D) No, thanks.

問題：帳單包含服務費嗎？

選項：(A) 麻煩帳單分開。

　　　(B) 這是你的小費。

　　　(C) 有的，10% 服務費。

　　　(D) 不，謝了。

---

23. Excuse me, how do I make a long-distance call from my room?

(A) I'd like to leave a message.

(B) Please dial "0" for emergency.

(C) First dial "9" and then dial the number.

(D) You can dial "2" for room service.

問題：不好意思，我要怎麼從我的房間打長途電話？

選項：(A) 我想要留言。

(B) 緊急情況請撥「零」。

(C) 先撥「九」，然後再撥號碼。

(D) 客房服務請撥「二」。

---

24. Is there a bookstore in your hotel?

(A) Yes. It's right down the hall.

(B) Sure. I'll send it to your room right away.

(C) I'm afraid you can't pay by credit card there.

(D) I'm sorry. The newspapers are sold out.

問題：你們的飯店裡有書店嗎？

選項：(A) 有的，就在大廳盡頭。

(B) 當然。我會立刻送到你房裡。

(C) 恐怕在那裡你不能以信用卡付款。

(D) 我很抱歉。報紙都賣完了。

提示：sell out 表示「賣完」。

---

25. Could you get a taxi for me?

(A) Sure. Wait a moment, please.

(B) Yes. You can find it in our store.

(C) Sorry. It'll be sent up right away.

(D) Please dial "9" for outside calls.

問題：可以幫我叫計程車嗎？

選項：(A) 當然。請稍等。

(B) 是的，你可以在我們的店裡找到它。

(C) 我很抱歉。立刻就送上去。

(D) 外線電話請撥「九」。

---

26. When does your first shuttle bus leave for the airport?

(A) Monday to Friday.

(B) 7:00 a.m. to 9:00 p.m.

(C) It's 2:30 p.m. now.

(D) 5:00 in the morning.

問題：你們第一班到機場的接駁巴士何時發車？

選項：(A) 週一至週五。

(B) 早上七點到晚上九點。

(C) 現在是下午兩點半。

(D) 早上五點。

---

27. Does the airport bus go to the Plaza Hotel downtown?

(A) No. It runs every half hour.

(B) Yes. It stops at all major hotels.

(C) Sure. Are you checking in now?

(D) Yes. Where are you heading for?

問題：這輛機場巴士會到市中心的 Plaza 飯店嗎？

選項：(A) 不會。它每半個小時一班。

(B) 會的。它會停所有主要的飯店。

(C) 當然。你現在要登記入住嗎？

(D) 會的。你要去哪裡？

---

28. Where can I rent a car?

(A) Please pay at that counter over there.

(B) It'll take you about 40 minutes.

(C) You'll need your passport and credit card for renting a car.

(D) Go straight ahead and you'll see the car rental desk on your left.

問題：我可以在哪裡租車？

選項：(A) 請到那邊那個櫃檯付款。

(B) 它將花你大約四十分鐘。

(C) 租車將需要你的護照和信用卡。

(D) 往前直走，你就會看到租車服務檯在你的左手邊。

---

29. How many nights are you planning to stay?

(A) Two double rooms, please.

(B) A trip to Hawaii sounds great.

(C) I'll stay in Spring Hotel. How about you?

(D) Six nights. Could you give me a discount?

問題：您打算住幾個晚上？

選項：(A) 麻煩兩間雙人房。

　　　(B) 到夏威夷旅行聽起來很棒。

　　　(C) 我會住在 Spring 飯店。你呢？

　　　(D) 六個晚上。你可以給我折扣嗎？

----

30. Are there any hostels near the airport?

(A) Yes, there are two within walking distance.

(B) Yes. It's 90 US dollars per night.

(C) Sounds OK. You can get there by shuttle bus.

(D) All rooms on the non-smoking floors are full.

問題：機場附近有任何旅社嗎？

選項：(A) 有的，有兩家走路就可以到。

　　　(B) 有的。一個晚上九十美元。

　　　(C) 聽起來不錯。你可以搭接駁巴士去那裡。

　　　(D) 所有在非吸菸樓層的房間都客滿了。

提示：within walking distance 意指「在走路可到的範圍裡」。

31. M: I'd like to copy these articles. Is there any copy machine on this floor?

W: No. You'll have to go down to the basement. We keep all our copy machines down there.

M: OK. And how much does it cost for one page?

W: One dollar. You can get change at the service counter down there.

Q: What is the man looking for?

(A) The service counter.

(B) Some change.

(C) A copy machine.

(D) Some magazine articles.

男：我想要影印這幾篇文章。這層樓有影印機嗎？

女：沒有。你必須到地下室。我們所有的影印機都設置在那裡。

男：好的。那印一頁多少錢呢？

女：一元。你可以在下面的服務檯換零錢。

問題：這位男子在找什麼？

選項：(A) 服務檯。

(B) 一些零錢。

(C) 一臺影印機。

(D) 一些雜誌文章。

32. W: Sir, the book you borrowed is overdue.

M: I'm sorry. I just couldn't get away until today.

W: I'm afraid you'll have to pay a fine.

M: How much is it?

W: Let me see. The fine is one NT dollar a day, and it's a total of ten days. It'll be ten NT dollars.

Q: Why was the man fined?

(A) He didn't buy a train ticket.

(B) He didn't return the library book on time.

(C) He didn't recycle his plastic bottles.

(D) He parked his car in the non-parking zone.

女：先生，你借的書逾期了。

男：我很抱歉。到今天以前我就是走不開。

女：恐怕你必須要付罰金。

男：那是多少呢？

女：讓我看看。逾期罰金是一天新臺幣一元，總共十天。罰金是新臺幣十元。

問題：這個男子為什麼被罰款？

選項：(A) 他沒買火車票。

(B) 他沒有準時還圖書館的書。

(C) 他沒有回收他的塑膠瓶。

(D) 他把他的車停在非停車區。

提示：get away 在此表示「走開，離開」。在對話當中的 fine 為名詞，表「罰金」之意；而問題中的 fine 則為動詞，表「罰款」之意。

---

33. W: What kind of novels do you like to read?

M: I like science fiction. I think they're really interesting. How about you?

W: I like science fiction, too, but I like historic novels even better.

Q: What kind of books does the woman like best?

(A) Science fiction.   (B) Detective stories.

(C) Historical novels.   (D) Romantic novels.

女：你喜歡讀哪一種小說？

男：我喜歡科幻小說。我覺得它們真的很有趣。你呢？

女：我也挺喜歡科幻小說的，但我更喜歡歷史小說。

問題：這個女子最喜歡哪一種書籍？

選項：(A) 科幻小說。   (B) 偵探故事。

(C) 歷史小說。   (D) 浪漫愛情小說。

34. W: I think this sofa would look nice in our apartment. What do you think?

M: Well, I like the style but not the color. Maybe we should pick a brown one instead of dark red.

W: You're right. Let's ask them and see if they have a brown one.

Q: Why does the man dislike the sofa?

(A) It is too small.

(B) Its color is not right.

(C) Its style is too old-fashioned.

(D) It is too expensive.

女：我覺得這個沙發椅在我們的公寓裡會很好看。你覺得呢？

男：嗯，我喜歡它的樣式，但不喜歡它的顏色。或許我們應該選個棕色的而非暗紅色的。

女：你是對的。讓我們問問看是否有棕色的。

問題：這位男子為什麼不喜歡這個沙發椅？

選項：(A) 它太小了。

(B) 它的顏色不對。

(C) 它的樣式太過時了。

(D) 它太貴了。

提示：old-fashioned 表「過時的，舊式的」。

35. M: I find my job very stressful. It takes almost all my time. I don't seem to have a personal life.

W: I'm sorry to hear that. How do you deal with your stress then?

M: I eat. I treat myself to a good restaurant every weekend.

Q: What is the cause of the man's stress?

(A) His personal life.　　(B) His job.

(C) His weight.　　　　　(D) His new restaurant.

男：我覺得我的工作非常地重。它幾乎花掉我全部的時間。我好像沒了自己的生活。

女：我很抱歉聽你這樣說。你都如何處理你的壓力呢？

男：我吃東西。我每個週末款待自己到一家好的餐廳吃飯。

問題：這個男子的壓力是什麼造成的？

選項：(A) 他的個人生活。

　　　(B) 他的工作。

　　　(C) 他的體重。

　　　(D) 他的新餐廳。

提示：deal with 表示「應付，處理」。

36. M: Do you have any questions concerning our

school?

W: Yes. I'd like to know about job opportunities on campus.

M: I think there are quite a few part-time jobs available on campus. The campus cafeteria, bookstore, or library often offers jobs to students.

Q: What are they talking about?

(A) Library rules.

(B) Job interviews.

(C) Cafeterias in schools.

(D) Available jobs on campus.

男：你有任何關於我們學校的問題嗎？

女：有的。我想知道有關校內的工作機會。

男：我想校內有不少可得的兼職工作。校內的自助餐館、書店或圖書館常提供工作給學生。

問題：他們在談什麼？

選項：(A) 圖書館規則。

　　　(B) 工作面試。

　　　(C) 學校裡的自助餐館。

　　　(D) 校內可得的工作。

提示：on campus 表示「校內」。

37. M: Have you thought about what club you're

going to join in college?

W: Yes. I'd like to join the Drama Club. In fact, I was the leader of my high school's Drama Club.

M: I see. So you must have experienced performing on stage.

W: That's for sure!

Q: What club did the woman join in high school?

(A) The Dance Club.　　(B) The Art Club.

(C) The Drama Club.　　(D) The Guitar Club.

男：你曾想過大學要加入哪種社團嗎？

女：有啊。我想要參加話劇社。事實上，我曾是高中話劇社社長。

男：我明白了。所以你一定有在臺上演出過。

女：那是當然的呀！

問題：這位女子在高中時參加過什麼社團？

選項：(A) 舞蹈社。　　(B) 美術社。

　　　(C) 話劇社。　　(D) 吉他社。

----

38. M: How's everything in your restaurant?

W: Not too good. My chef quit yesterday and I'm desperate to find somebody who can cook Italian food.

M: Ah, my cousin just graduated from cooking school. Maybe you'd like to talk to him.

W: That'd be great. Thanks a lot.

Q: What does the woman do?

(A) She is a chef.

(B) She is a graduate student.

(C) She is a teacher in a cooking school.

(D) She is a restaurant owner.

男：你的餐廳一切都好嗎？

女：不太好。我的主廚昨天辭職了，而我現在急著要找到一個會煮義大利菜的人。

男：啊，我的表弟剛從烹飪學校畢業。或許你會想和他談一下。

女：那真是太棒了。太謝謝你了。

問題：這位女子是做什麼的？

選項：(A) 她是位研究生。

　　　(B) 她是位主廚。

　　　(C) 她是位烹飪學校的老師。

　　　(D) 她是位餐廳老闆。

提示：女子說她的主廚辭職了，而且她急著找新廚師，所以她可能是該餐廳的負責人。

....

39. W: It was very brave of you to stop the bank robber today.

M: Oh, I was just doing my job.

W: How did you feel when you caught him?

M: I felt relieved. And I'm glad nobody was hurt.

Q: What do you think the man is?

(A) A police officer.　　(B) A doctor.

(C) A professor.　　(D) A reporter.

女：你今天非常勇敢地阻止了那名銀行搶匪。

男：喔，我只是盡我的職責。

女：當你逮捕他的時候感覺如何？

男：我感到放心。而且我很高興沒有人受傷。

問題：你覺得這位男子是做什麼的？

選項：(A) 警察。　　(B) 醫生。

　　　(C) 教授。　　(D) 記者。

40. W: Tim, why don't we go to Spain for our vacation? We haven't been to that part of the world.

M: But Jenny, one thing we should think about is we don't know the language.

W: Right. That's always a problem. Let's think of other places then.

Q: Why didn't Tim agree to go to Spain?

(A) Tim has already been to Spain.

(B) Neither Tim nor Jenny can speak Spanish.

(C) Spain is too far to travel to.

(D) Other places are cheaper to visit.

女：Tim，我們何不到西班牙去渡假？我們還沒去過
那裡。

男：但是 Jenny，我們應該考慮到語言不通的問題。

女：對耶。那總是個問題。讓我們想想其他地方吧。

問題：為什麼 Tim 不同意去西班牙？

選項：(A) Tim 已經去過西班牙了。

(B) Tim 和 Jenny 都不會說西班牙語。

(C) 去西班牙旅行太遠了。

(D) 去其他地方渡假比較便宜。

提示：Tim 說的語言指的就是西班牙語。

- -

41. W: Do you have any plans for the coming New
Year's vacation?

M: Yes. My family and I are going to Australia.

W: Wow! I heard the scenery there is amazing. I
wish I had the money to go.

Q: Which is NOT true?

(A) Australia has beautiful scenery.

(B) The man is going to Australia.

(C) The man has no plans for his New Year's
vacation.

⑩ The woman has no money to go to
　　Australia.

女：你對即將到來的新年假期有計畫嗎？

男：有啊。我和我的家人要去澳洲。

女：哇！我聽說那裡的自然景觀非常驚人。我希望我
　　有錢可以去。

問題：何者不屬實？

選項：⒜ 澳洲有美麗的景觀。

　　　⒝ 男子將要去澳洲。

　　　⒞ 男子對新年假期沒有計畫。

　　　⒟ 女子沒有錢去澳洲。

- -

42. M: What's bothering you?

　　W: Oh, nothing important. It's just that I can't
　　　　decide whether I should go to Mt. Ali or
　　　　Hualien for the holiday.

　　M: I went by train to Mt. Ali last month. The
　　　　forest and the sunrise were beautiful. I really
　　　　enjoyed it. But I've never been to Hualien.
　　　　I'd really like to go there someday.

　　Q: What did the man NOT do when he went
　　　　to Mt. Ali?

　　⒜ Ride the train.

　　⒝ Enjoy the hot springs.

(C) See the forest.

(D) See the sunrise.

男：你在煩什麼？

女：喔，沒什麼重要的。就只是我無法決定放假應該
　　要去阿里山還是花蓮。

男：上個月我搭火車到阿里山，那裡的森林和日出都
　　很美，我真的非常享受。但是我還沒去過花蓮，
　　我真的很想哪天可以去那裡。

問題：這個男子去阿里山時，他沒有做哪件事？

選項：(A) 搭火車。　　(B) 享受溫泉。

　　　(C) 看森林。　　(D) 賞日出。

---

43. W: Holiday Hotel. May I help you?

M: Yes. I'd like to know if you have any
   vacancies from May 4th to 6th.

W: Let me check...yes, we do.

M: Would you reserve three double rooms for
   me, please?

Q: How many rooms does the man want to
   book?

(A) Three.　　(B) Four.　　(C) Five.　　(D) Six.

女：Holiday 旅館，我能為您服務嗎？

男：是的，我想知道你們從五月五日到六日是否有空
　　房？

女：讓我看看……有，我們有空房。

男：那可以請你幫我預留三間雙人房嗎？

問題：這個男子要訂幾間房？

選項：(A) 三間。　　　(B) 四間。

　　　(C) 五間。　　　(D) 六間。

---

44. M: OK, it's all set. You'll be leaving on July
    23rd, and returning on July 30th.

    W: That's right. By the way, is it possible to
    reserve a seat now?

    M: Sure. What kind of seat do you prefer?

    W: Aisle seat, please.

    Q: When will the woman be back?

    (A) June 20th. 　　　(B) July 30th.

    (C) June 13th. 　　　(D) July 23rd.

    男：好了，都訂好了。您將於 7 月 23 日啟程，並於
    7 月 30 日回來。

    女：沒錯。順便問一下，現在能夠預約座位嗎？

    男：當然。您喜歡怎樣的位子？

    女：麻煩靠走道的位子。

    問題：這位女子將何時回來？

    選項：(A) 6 月 20 日。　　(B) 7 月 30 日。

    　　　(C) 6 月 13 日。　　(D) 7 月 23 日。

45. W: I'm sorry, sir. This flight is fully booked.

M: Oh, no! I really have to get on this flight to Berlin. Could you check the business class or first class for me?

W: Let me see. Oh, there's a seat in the business class.

M: Great. I'll take it.

Q: Where will this man sit on the flight to Berlin?

(A) In the first class.

(B) In the business class.

(C) In the economy class.

(D) None of the above.

女：很抱歉，先生，這班飛機已經客滿了。

男：喔，不！我真的必須搭上這班往柏林的飛機。你能幫我查查商務艙或頭等艙嗎？

女：讓我看看。喔，商務艙有一個位子。

男：太好了。我要了。

問題：在往柏林的飛機上，這名男子將坐在哪裡？

選項：(A) 在頭等艙裡。　　(B) 在商務艙裡。

　　　(C) 在經濟艙裡。　　(D) 以上皆非。

提示：飛機的艙等通常分成三種：first class「頭等艙」、business class「商務艙」和 economy class「經濟艙」。

Test 2

此部分有 15 題，每題都有一張與該題目相對應的圖畫。請聽錄音機播出題目以及 A、B、C、D 四個英語敘述之後，選出與所看到的圖畫最相符的答案。每題只播出一遍。

Come and join
the Japanese Club
to study the language
and Japanese culture!

1st Tuesday of each month
Cost: $100/per month

College Admission
Interview

4 _____

5 _____

DEPARTURE

Scheduled Time	New Time	Destination
08:10	08:25	London
08:40	09:00	Bangkok
09:10		Bali
10:05	10:20	Sydney
10:25		Hong Kong

6 _____

Foreign Exchange Application Form

Name: _Mary Huang_

ID No: _A374628765_

Currency:

☒ US Dollars ☐ Other: _____

Type/Amount:

☐ Cash: _____

☒ Traveler's Check: _US$1,000_

7 _____

8 ____

9 ____

10 ____

Hotel Service	Extension
General Info	0
Housekeeping	9
Lost & Found	8
Room Service	1
Mail & Message	6

11 ____

12 _____

13 _____

14 _____

15 _____

此部分有 15 題，每題請聽錄音機播出一個英語
句子之後，從 A、B、C、D 四個回答或回應中，
選出一個最適合者作答。每題只播出一遍。

_____ 16 (A) Sure. I'll notify you as soon as it's
returned.
(B) No problem. Just call me when
you're free.
(C) OK. I don't really like the book
anyway.
(D) I'm sorry. We're fully booked this
Saturday.

_____ 17 (A) It looks nice but it's too
expensive.
(B) I think you look great in that
dress.
(C) It's nothing. Don't mention it.
(D) I think your idea is brilliant.

_____ 18 (A) I'm sorry. Smoking is not allowed
here.

(B) There's a smoking area around the corner.

(C) I think it's great that warning signs are printed on cigarette packets.

(D) I think it's good news for people who don't smoke like me.

19 (A) I'm sure your sons will remember your birthday.

(B) Maybe you should move to a smaller apartment.

(C) Do you want me to give you a ride home?

(D) Why don't you take a couple of days off?

20 (A) Yes, this is a new dish.

(B) Sure. I'll be right back.

(C) I'd like a coffee, please.

(D) Sorry for the trouble.

21 (A) I like seeing movies.

(B) I like action movies.

(C) I don't like rock music.

(D) I prefer going to the theater.

22 (A) I feel much better, thanks.

(B) It's 45 pounds to 1 NT dollar.

(C) In small bills or large bills?

(D) I'm sorry. These rates are fixed.

23 (A) How much do you pay for it?

(B) Why don't you change your job?

(C) I'm glad to hear that.

(D) So far so good.

24 (A) Yes, it's Amy's.

(B) No, thank you.

(C) No. Mine is here.

(D) Yes. I'd love to.

25 (A) Sorry. I don't think so.

(B) I think it's quite reasonable.

(C) Well, you have a point there.

(D) I'm not so sure about it.

26 (A) I think we can rent a car.

(B) I'm sure it's a good idea.

(C) I heard the sky is incredibly blue there.

(D) Let's buy some food at the local

market.

27 (A) I'd like two double rooms, please.

(B) I think I'll stay for three nights.

(C) I really appreciate your help.

(D) Well, I'd prefer a three-star hotel.

28 (A) I'll try to be there on time.

(B) I checked in just now.

(C) It's 10:00 tomorrow moring.

(D) It's already half past six.

29 (A) Sure. I'll see what I can do.

(B) Here're your boarding passes.

(C) Are you checking in together?

(D) May I have your passports and tickets?

30 (A) Sure. Here you go.

(B) Yes. Here's my passport.

(C) I'm from Taiwan.

(D) I don't have a driver's license.

Track #06

此部分有 15 題，每題請聽錄音機播出一段對話及一個相關的問題，然後從 A、B、C、D 四個選項中挑出一個最適合的答案。每題只播出一遍。

_____ 31 (A) One.　　　　(B) Two.
(C) Three.　　　(D) Four.

_____ 32 (A) Move his bag to another compartment.
(B) Buy duty-free with his checks.
(C) Change to a window seat.
(D) Change to an aisle seat.

_____ 33 (A) In 100-dollar and 20-dollar bills.
(B) In 50-dollar and 20-dollar bills.
(C) In 100-dollar and 50-dollar bills.
(D) In 10-dollar and 50-dollar bills.

_____ 34 (A) 200 US dollars.
(B) 300 US dollars.
(C) 400 US dollars.
(D) None of the above.

_____ 35 (A) She was given wrong directions.

(B) She lost her sense of direction.

(C) The airport signs were unclear.

(D) There were too many bus lines.

36 (A) On the fifth floor.

(B) On the seventh floor.

(C) On the eighth floor.

(D) On the ninth floor.

37 (A) $0.

(B) $240.

(C) $480.

(D) None of the above.

38 (A) $1,000.   (B) $1,100.

(C) $2,000.   (D) $2,200.

39 (A) Her steak was not well-done.

(B) Her chicken was overcooked

(C) She was given the wrong change.

(D) She wasn't given the correct bill.

40 (A) One more day.

(B) Two more days.

(C) Three more days.

(D) Four more days.

41 (A) Paul quit his job at the hospital.

(B) Paul was taken to the hospital.

(C) Paul's father fell down in the hospital.

(D) Paul's father got hurt during the shower.

42 (A) By special delivery.

(B) By surface mail.

(C) By airmail.

(D) By registered mail.

43 (A) It was past the lunch time.

(B) He didn't have a reservation.

(C) He didn't see the sign at the door.

(D) He wasn't dressed properly.

44 (A) He broke his arm.

(B) He was cut by a broken pot.

(C) He was burned by boiling water.

(D) He was nearly drowned.

45 (A) A wedding party.

(B) Bad food.

(C) Pressure from work.

(D) Bad weather.

Track #04

1. What is the man saying to the woman?
   (A) The food tastes delicious.
   (B) Thank you for your help.
   (C) I don't think I ordered this.
   (D) Let me treat you to dinner.
   問題：這個男子正在對女子說什麼？
   選項：(A) 這食物嚐起來很美味。
   　　　(B) 謝謝你的幫忙。
   　　　(C) 我不認為我點了這個。
   　　　(D) 讓我請你吃晚餐。

. . . .

2. How often do the members meet for the study?
   (A) Once a week.　　　(B) Twice a week.
   (C) Once a month.　　 (D) Twice a month.
   問題：這個社團的成員多常聚會？
   選項：(A) 每週一次。　　(B) 每週兩次。
   　　　(C) 每月一次。　　(D) 每月兩次。
   提示：聚會時間為每個月的第一個星期二，故一個月
   　　　一次。

. . . .

3. What do you think the girl is saying?

(A) What school are you from?

(B) What would you like to drink?

(C) I'd like to have one ticket.

(D) My name is Chen Ling-ling.

問題：你認為這個女生正在說什麼？

選項：(A) 你來自哪所學校？

(B) 你想要喝什麼？

(C) 我要買一張票。

(D) 我的名字是陳凌伶。

---

4. What is the man doing?

(A) Going through security.

(B) Buying food at a café.

(C) Checking in at the airport.

(D) Boarding a plane.

問題：這個男子在做什麼？

選項：(A) 通過安檢。

(B) 在咖啡館買食物。

(C) 辦理登機手續。

(D) 登機。

---

5. What time will the plane take off for Sydney?

(A) 9:35.　　　　　　　(B) 10:05.

(C) 10:20.　　　　　　　(D) 10:25.

問題：往雪梨的班機幾點起飛？

選項：(A) 9 點 35 分。　　(B) 10 點 5 分。

　　　(C) 10 點 20 分。　(D) 10 點 25 分。

....

6. What will Mary receive from the bank?

(A) A check.　　　　　(B) Some cash.

(C) 100 US dollars.　　(D) Traveler's checks.

問題：Mary 會從銀行拿到什麼？

選項：(A) 一張支票。　　(B) 一些現金。

　　　(C) 美金一百元。　(D) 旅行支票。

提示：Mary 要申請一千美元的旅行支票。

....

7. What does the man want to know?

(A) Information about opening an account.

(B) Foreign currency exchange rate.

(C) How to apply for a credit card.

(D) Where he can cash a check.

問題：這個男子想要知道什麼？

選項：(A) 有關開戶的資訊。

　　　(B) 外幣匯率。

　　　(C) 如何申請信用卡。

　　　(D) 他可以在哪裡兌現支票。

提示：account 在此指的是銀行帳戶。cash 在此為
動詞，表示「兌現」。

8. What was the woman's question?

(A) What is the exchange rate for Japanese Yen today?

(B) How much Japanese Yen do you want to change?

(C) Can I change US dollars into NT dollars?

(D) Do you have any NT dollars now?

問題：這個女子在詢問哪一種外幣？

選項：(A) 今天日幣的匯率是多少？

　　　(B) 你要兌換多少日圓？

　　　(C) 我可以將美元兌換成新臺幣嗎？

　　　(D) 你現在有任何新臺幣嗎？

9. How much time is left before the health club closes?

(A) Half an hour.

(B) One and a half hours.

(C) Two hours.

(D) Two and a half hours.

問題：距離這家健身中心打烊還有多少時間？

選項：(A) 半小時。　　　(B) 一個半小時。

　　　(C) 兩小時。　　　(D) 兩個半小時。

提示：八點到九點半尚有一個半小時的時間。

10. What number should you dial if you find your jacket missing?

(A) 0.　　　(B) 1.　　　(C) 6.　　　(D) 8.

問題：如果你發現你的夾克不見了，你應該撥哪個號碼？

選項：(A) 零。　(B) 一。　(C) 六。　(D) 八。

提示：general info「一般資訊」；housekeeping/ laundry「房務與洗衣服務」；Lost & Found「失物招領」；room service「客房服務」。

---

11. How does the man want his package to be sent?

(A) By surface mail.　　(B) By express.

(C) By airmail.　　(D) None of the above.

問題：這位男子想要如何郵寄他的包裹？

選項：(A) 以普通平信的方式。

　　　(B) 以快遞的方式。

　　　(C) 以航空郵件的方式。

　　　(D) 以上皆非。

---

12. What did the man ask the woman?

(A) Where would you send it?

(B) What's wrong with it?

(C) What's inside?

(D) How would you like to send it?

問題：這名男子問了這位女子什麼？

選項：(A) 要寄到哪裡？

　　　(B) 它怎麼了？

　　　(C) 裡面是什麼？

　　　(D) 要以什麼方式寄送？

---

13. Who is the sender?

(A) Sara.　　　　　　　(B) Sanmin.

(C) Saratoga.　　　　　(D) Henry.

問題：寄件者是誰？

選項：(A) Sara。　　　　(B) Sanmin。

　　　(C) Saratoga。　　(D) Henry。

提示：西式信封的寄件人姓名和住址寫在左上欄。

---

14. What is happening?

(A) Someone is smoking.

(B) Someone is jumping down.

(C) A building is on fire.

(D) A truck is burning fiercely.

問題：發生什麼事？

選項：(A) 有人正在抽菸。

　　　(B) 有人在往下跳。

(C) 大樓失火了。

(D) 卡車正熊熊燃燒。

---

15. Which is true?

(A) Two cars bumped into each other.

(B) No one is hurt in the accident.

(C) The car driver hit someone and ran.

(D) None of the above.

問題：何者屬實？

選項：(A) 兩輛汽車相撞。

　　　(B) 事故中無人受傷。

　　　(C) 汽車駕駛撞人逃逸。

　　　(D) 以上皆非。

第二部分　腳本與解析　 Track #05

16. Could you reserve that book for me?

(A) Sure. I'll notify you as soon as it's returned.

(B) No problem. Just call me when you're free.

(C) OK. I don't really like the book anyway.

(D) I'm sorry. We're fully booked this Saturday.

問題：你可以幫我預留那本書嗎？

選項：(A) 當然。它一被歸還我就會立刻通知你。

(B) 沒問題。等你有空再打給我就好。

(C) 好吧。反正我也不真的喜歡那本書。

(D) 我很抱歉。這週六我們都客滿了。

---

17. How does this coat look to you?

(A) It looks nice but it's too expensive.

(B) I think you look great in that dress.

(C) It's nothing. Don't mention it.

(D) I think your idea is brilliant.

問題：你覺得這件大衣看起來如何？

選項：(A) 看起來挺好的但就是太貴。

(B) 我覺得你穿那件洋裝很好看。

(C) 那沒什麼。不用客氣。

(D) 我覺得你的想法好極了。

---

18. What is your view on the recent ban on smoking in all public places?

(A) I'm sorry. Smoking is not allowed here.

(B) There's a smoking area around the corner.

(C) I think it's great that warning signs are printed on cigarette packets.

(D) I think it's good news for people who don't smoke like me.

問題：你對最近所有公共場所禁止吸煙有什麼看法？

選項：(A) 我很抱歉。這裡禁止吸菸。

(B) 角落那裡有吸菸區。

(C) 我認為在香菸盒上印製警告標誌很好。

(D) 我想這對像我一樣不抽菸的人來說是好消息。

提示：ban on...「對……的禁止」。ban 在此為名詞，它也可以是及物動詞。

---

19. My house feels kind of empty since my two sons moved out.

(A) I'm sure your sons will remember your birthday.

(B) Maybe you should move to a smaller apartment.

(C) Do you want me to give you a ride home?

(D) Why don't you take a couple of days off?

問題：因為我的兩個兒子搬出去了，房子感覺有點空。

選項：(A) 我確信你的兒子們會記得你的生日。

(B) 或許你應該搬到較小的公寓。

(C) 你要我送你回家嗎？

(D) 你為何不請幾天假呢？

提示：give sb a ride 表「載某人一程」。

20. Could I trouble you to bring me your menu again?

    (A) Yes, this is a new dish.

    (B) Sure. I'll be right back.

    (C) I'd like a coffee, please.

    (D) Sorry for the trouble.

    問題：可以麻煩你再給我一次你們的菜單嗎？

    選項：(A) 是的，這是新菜。

          (B) 當然。我立刻就回來。

          (C) 麻煩給我一杯咖啡。

          (D) 抱歉造成您的麻煩。

21. What kind of movies do you like?

    (A) I like seeing movies.

    (B) I like action movies.

    (C) I don't like rock music.

    (D) I prefer going to the theater.

    問題：你喜歡哪種電影？

    選項：(A) 我喜歡看電影。

          (B) 我喜歡動作片。

          (C) 我不喜歡搖滾樂。

          (D) 我偏好去電影院。

22. Could you give me a better rate?

(A) I feel much better, thanks.

(B) It's 45 pounds to 1 NT dollar.

(C) In small bills or large bills?

(D) I'm sorry. These rates are fixed.

問題：你可以給我個比較好的價格嗎？

選項：(A) 我覺得好多了，謝謝。

　　　(B) 45 英鎊對新臺幣 1 元。

　　　(C) 小鈔還是大鈔？

　　　(D) 抱歉，這些價格都是固定的。

提示：rate 有「比率」或「價格」的意思。

---

23. My new job pays much better than my old one.

(A) How much do you pay for it?

(B) Why don't you change your job?

(C) I'm glad to hear that.

(D) So far so good.

問題：我新工作的給薪比舊的好多了。

選項：(A) 你付多少錢？

　　　(B) 你何不換工作？

　　　(C) 我很高興聽你這麼說。

　　　(D) 到目前為止還好。

---

24. Is this your bag?

(A) Yes, it's Amy's.　　　(B) No, thank you.

(C) No. Mine is here.   (D) Yes. I'd love to.

問題：這是你的袋子嗎？

選項：(A) 對，是 Amy 的。

　　　(B) 不了，謝謝你。

　　　(C) 不是，我的在這。

　　　(D) 好啊，我很樂意。

---

25. How does this price for the Thai package tour sound to you?

(A) Sorry, I don't think so.

(B) I think it's quite reasonable.

(C) Well, you have a point there.

(D) I'm not so sure about it.

問題：你覺得這個泰國套裝行程的價格聽起來如何？

選項：(A) 抱歉，我不這麼認為。

　　　(B) 我認為還挺合理的。

　　　(C) 好吧，你說的有理。

　　　(D) 我不太確定。

---

26. How do we get around in Spain?

(A) I think we can rent a car.

(B) I'm sure it's a good idea.

(C) I heard the sky is incredibly blue there.

(D) Let's buy some food at the local market.

問題：我們要如何在西班牙旅遊？

選項：(A) 我想我們可以租輛車。

(B) 我確定這是個好主意。

(C) 我聽說那裡的天空極藍。

(D) 讓我們在當地市場買點食物。

提示：get around 表示「到處走動」。

---

27. How about youth hostels? They're cheaper.

(A) I'd like two double rooms, please.

(B) I think I'll stay for three nights.

(C) I really appreciate your help.

(D) Well, I'd prefer a three-star hotel.

問題：青年旅館如何？它們比較便宜。

選項：(A) 我想要兩間雙人房。

(B) 我想我要住三個晚上。

(C) 我非常感謝你的幫忙。

(D) 喔，我寧願選擇三星級的飯店。

---

28. What is your check-out time?

(A) I'll try to be there on time.

(B) I checked in just now.

(C) It's 10:00 tomorrow morning.

(D) It's already half past six.

問題：你們的退房時間是幾點？

選項：(A) 我會試著準時到的。

(B) 我剛辦好入宿登記。

(C) 明天早上十點。

(D) 現在已經六點半了。

提示：最後一個選項應該是用來回答現在幾點。

---

29. Is it possible to give us an aisle seat and the seat next to it?

(A) Sure. I'll see what I can do.

(B) Here're your boarding passes.

(C) Are you checking in together?

(D) May I have your passports and tickets?

問題：能夠給我們一個靠走道的位子以及它旁邊的位子嗎？

選項：(A) 當然，讓我看看我能做什麼。

(B) 這是你們的登機證。

(C) 你們要一起辦理登機嗎？

(D) 可以給我你們的護照和機票嗎？

提示：這裡的 check in 指的是到機場櫃檯報到，辦理登機手續。

---

30. May I see your return ticket, please?

(A) Sure. Here you go.

(B) Yes. Here's my passport.

(C) I'm from Taiwan.

(D) I don't have a driver's license.

問題：麻煩讓我看一下你回程的票好嗎？

選項：(A) 當然。拿去吧。

　　　(B) 好的。這是我的護照。

　　　(C) 我從臺灣來。

　　　(D) 我沒有駕駛執照。

第三部分　腳本與解析

Track #06

31. W: How many pieces of baggage are you checking in?

M: These two cases.

W: Do you have any hand baggage?

M: Yes. Just one.

Q: How many pieces of baggage did the man check in?

(A) One.　　　　　　(B) Two.

(C) Three.　　　　　(D) Four.

女：您有幾件行李要登記託運？

男：這兩箱。

女：您有任何手提行李嗎？

男：是的，只有一件。

問題：這個男子登記拖運了幾件行李？

選項：(A) 一件。   (B) 兩件。

      (C) 三件。   (D) 四件。

---

32. M: Excuse me. I was wondering if I could move to an aisle seat.

W: This plane is quite full. I'm not sure if there're any aisle seats left.

M: Would you please check for me? This window seat is very inconvenient.

W: OK. Please wait a moment.

Q: What does the man want to do?

(A) Move his bag to another compartment.

(B) Buy duty-free with his checks

(C) Change to a window seat.

(D) Change to an aisle seat.

男：不好意思，我在想是否能夠移到靠走道的座位。

女：這班飛機乘客挺多的。我不確定是否留有任何靠走道的座位。

男：可以麻煩你看一下嗎？靠窗的位子非常不方便。

女：好的。請稍等。

問題：這個男子想要什麼？

選項：(A) 將他的包包移到另一個行李架。

      (B) 用他的支票買免稅商品。

(C) 換到靠窗的座位。

(D) 換到靠走道的座位。

提示：duty-free 作形容詞用時表「免稅的」，作名詞
時則為「免稅商品」，通常為不可數。

---

33. W: Here's my passport. I'll sign the checks now.

M: Great. Do you want it all in 100-dollar bills?

W: Please give me ten 100-dollar bills and the
rest in 50-dollar bills.

M: No problem. One moment, please.

Q: How does the woman want her money?

(A) In 100-dollar and 20-dollar bills.

(B) In 50-dollar and 20-dollar bills.

(C) In 100-dollar and 50-dollar bills.

(D) In 10-dollar and 50-dollar bills.

女：這是我的護照。我現在就簽這些支票。

男：好極了。你要全部都是百元鈔票嗎？

女：麻煩給我十張百元鈔票，其他都是五十元鈔票。

男：沒問題。請稍等。

問題：這位女子要怎麼換她的錢？

選項：(A) 百元和二十元鈔票。

(B) 五十元和二十元鈔票。

(C) 百元和五十元鈔票。

(D) 十元和五十元鈔票。

34. W: Could I cash some traveler's checks here?

M: Yes. But our bank doesn't take more than 200 US dollars.

W: Is there a service charge?

M: No. But you have to show us your passport or ID.

Q: How much can the woman cash traveler's checks at this bank?

(A) 200 US dollars.　　(B) 300 US dollars.

(C) 400 US dollars.　　(D) None of the above.

女：我可以在這裡兌現旅行支票嗎？

男：可以，但我們銀行不接受兩百美元以上的交易。

女：有服務費嗎？

男：沒有。但你必須出示你的護照或身分證件。

問題：這個女子可以在這家銀行兌現多少旅行支票？

選項：(A) 兩百美元。　　(B) 三百美元。

　　　(C) 四百美元。　　(D) 以上皆非。

35. W: Hi, I noticed that there are several different buses traveling from the airport to the city center. It's kind of confusing for me.

M: Just tell me where you want to go, and I'll show you which one to take.

W: Fine. I want to go to the Pearl Hotel on Harbor Road.

M: Just a minute. OK, you can take either Bus No. 7 or No. 10.

Q: Why was the woman confused?

(A) She was given wrong directions.

(B) She lost her sense of direction.

(C) The airport signs were unclear.

(D) There were too many bus lines.

女：你好，我注意到從機場到市中心有好多不同的公車。我有些困惑。

男：只要告訴我你要去哪裡，我會告訴你可以搭乘的車。

女：好吧。我要去 Harbor 路上的 Pearl 飯店。

男：稍等。好的，你可以搭七號或十號公車。

問題：這個女子為什麼感到困惑？

選項：(A) 她被指引錯方向。

　　　(B) 她失去了方向感。

　　　(C) 機場的標示不清楚。

　　　(D) 有太多公車路線。

提示：sense of direction 意為「方向感」。

⋯⋯⋯⋯⋯⋯⋯⋯⋯⋯⋯⋯⋯⋯⋯⋯⋯⋯⋯⋯⋯⋯

36. M: By the way, do you have a gym in the hotel?

W: Yes, we do. It's on the fifth floor, the same

floor as the swimming pool.

M: That's great. What time does the gym open?

W: 7 a.m. to 8 p.m. Have a nice day.

Q: Where is the hotel's swimming pool?

(A) On the fifth floor.

(B) On the seventh floor.

(C) On the eighth floor.

(D) On the ninth floor.

男：順便問一下，你們飯店裡有健身房嗎？

女：有的。它在飯店的五樓，和游泳池同一層樓。

男：好極了。健身房幾點開放？

女：早上七點至晚上八點。祝您有愉快的一天。

問題：飯店的游泳池在哪裡？

選項：(A) 在五樓。　　　(B) 在七樓。

　　　(C) 在八樓。　　　(D) 在九樓。

提示：游泳池和健身房在同一層樓。

- -

37. W: Let me get the bill, please.

M: Are you sure you don't want to go Dutch?

W: No. It's only $480. You can get it next time.

M: OK, thanks. Let's meet up again soon.

Q: How much will the woman pay?

(A) $0.　　　　　　　　(B) $240.

(C) $480.　　　　　　　(D) None of the above.

女：請讓我付帳。

男：你確定你不想各自付帳嗎？

女：不了。就只是 480 元。下次可以換你付。

男：好吧，謝了。那我們近期再聚聚吧。

問題：這個女子將付多少錢？

選項：(A) 0 元。　　　　　(B) 240 元。

　　　(C) 480 元。　　　　(D) 以上皆非。

---

38. M: Let me get the bill.

W: How much is it?

M: $2,000, including a 10% service charge.

W: Why don't we split the cost? I'll feel better if we do.

M: All right. If you insist.

Q: How much will the man pay?

(A) $1,000.　　　　　　(B) $1,100.

(C) $2,000.　　　　　　(D) $2,200.

男：讓我來付。

女：多少錢？

男：兩千元，含一成服務費。

女：何不自付各的？這樣的話我會覺得好過點。

男：好吧，如果你堅持的話。

問題：這個男子將付多少錢？

選項：(A) 1,000 元。　　　(B) 1,100 元。

(C) 2,000 元。　　(D) 2,200 元。

───────────────────────────────

39. W: Excuse me. I think you gave us the wrong
bill.

M: Oh, could you tell me what the problem is?

W: Sure. For example, we didn't order New
York steak or chicken special.

M: Let me see. Oh, I'm terribly sorry. This bill is
for another table.

Q: What is the woman's problem?

(A) Her steak was not well-done.

(B) Her chicken was overcooked

(C) She was given the wrong change.

(D) She wasn't given the correct bill.

女：不好意思。我想你給錯帳單了。

男：喔，可以告訴我有什麼問題嗎？

女：當然。比方說我們並沒有點紐約牛排或雞肉特
餐。

男：讓我看看。喔，我非常地抱歉。這是另一桌的帳
單。

問題：這個女子的問題是什麼？

選項：(A) 她的牛排不是全熟。

(B) 她的雞肉煮過頭了。

(C) 她被找錯錢了。

(D) 她沒有拿到對的帳單。

---

40. M: Ms. Lin, do you feel better today?

W: Yes, I do. Thanks.

M: I'll give you some medicine for the next three days. If you feel OK after three days, you don't have to come back for another checkup.

Q: How much longer will the woman take the medicine?

(A) One more day.　　(B) Two more days.

(C) Three more days.　　(D) Four more days.

男：林小姐，你今天覺得好多了嗎？

女：是的。謝謝。

男：我會開之後三天的藥給你。三天之後如果你覺得沒事了，你就不必再回來複檢了。

問題：這個女子將再服多久的藥？

選項：(A) 再一天。　　(B) 再兩天。

　　　(C) 再三天。　　(D) 再四天。

提示：checkup 表示「(身體)檢查」。

---

41. W: Paul, you look worried. What's wrong?

M: My father was sent to the hospital yesterday.

W: What happened?

M: He fell while he was taking a shower.

W: Oh, I'm sorry to hear that. Is he OK?

Q: What are they talking about?

(A) Paul quit his job at the hospital.

(B) Paul was taken to the hospital.

(C) Paul's father fell down in the hospital.

(D) Paul's father got hurt during the shower.

女：Paul，你看起來很擔憂。怎麼了嗎？

男：我父親昨天被送進醫院。

女：發生什麼事了？

男：他在洗澡時摔倒了。

女：喔，我很抱歉。他現在還好嗎？

問題：他們在談什麼？

選項：(A) Paul 決定辭掉他在醫院的工作。

(B) Paul 昨天被送進醫院。

(C) Paul 的父親在醫院摔倒。

(D) Paul 的父親在洗澡時受傷了。

---

42. M: Hi, I'd like to send this book to the United States.

W: Sure. How would you like to send it?

M: By airmail, please. Is there a special rate for printed matter?

W: Yes, let me see. That'll be NT$250.

Q: How is the man's book going to be sent?

(A) By special delivery.　(B) By surface mail.

(C) By airmail.　(D) By registered mail.

男：你好，我想要寄這本書到美國。

女：沒問題。你想要怎麼寄它呢？

男：麻煩以航空郵遞。印刷品有特別的價格嗎？

女：有的，讓我看看。那會是 250 元。

問題：這個男子的書將會被如何寄送？

選項：(A) 以特別郵遞。　(B) 以平信。

　　　(C) 以航空郵遞。　(D) 以掛號信。

提示：printed matter 指的是「印刷品」。

---

43. W: I'm sorry, sir. I'm afraid you can't go inside.

M: Why? I'd like to have lunch here.

W: Yes. But you missed the sign at the door. It says, "No Sandals or Shorts, please."

M: Oh, I'm sorry. I didn't see it.

Q: Why was the man not allowed to enter the restaurant?

(A) It was past the lunch time.

(B) He didn't have a reservation.

(C) He didn't see the sign at the door.

(D) He wasn't dressed properly.

女：對不起，先生。您恐怕不能進入。

男：為什麼？我想要在這裡吃午餐。

女：是的，但是你沒看見門口的標示。上面寫著「請勿著涼鞋或短褲」。

男：喔，我很抱歉。我沒看見。

問題：為何這位男子不被允許進入這家餐廳？

選項：(A) 他沒有預約。

(B) 午餐時間過了。

(C) 他沒有看見門口的標示。

(D) 他沒有穿著合宜。

---

44. M: General Hospital. May I help you?

W: My son accidentally knocked over a pot of boiling water and burned his arm. What shall I do?

M: Calm down, ma'am. First place his arm under running cold water. Now give me your address and I'll send an ambulance right over.

Q: What happened to the woman's son?

(A) He broke his arm.

(B) He was cut by a broken pot.

(C) He was burned by boiling water.

(D) He was nearly drowned.

男：General 醫院，我能為您效勞嗎？

女：我兒子不小心打翻了一壺滾燙的水，並燙傷了他的手臂。我該怎麼做？

男：冷靜，女士。首先將他的手臂置於流動的冷水下。現在給我您的住址，我會立刻派救護車過去。

問題：這個女子的兒子怎麼了？

選項：(A) 他的手臂斷了。

(B) 他被破掉的水壺割傷了。

(C) 他被滾水燙傷了。

(D) 他差點溺斃了。

提示：knock over「撞倒，打翻」；running「(水)流動的」。

---

45. M: I feel like throwing up, doctor.

W: What did you eat?

M: I was at a wedding party a couple of hours ago. Maybe it was because of the fish. It smelt weird.

Q: What caused the man to feel uncomfortable?

(A) A wedding party.　　(B) Bad food.

(C) Pressure from work.　(D) Bad weather.

男：醫生，我想吐。

女：你吃了什麼東西？

男：幾個小時前我參加了一場婚宴。可能是因為那道

魚，它聞起來怪怪的。

問題：是什麼造成了這個男子不舒服？

選項：(A) 一場婚宴。　　　(B) 不好的食物。

　　　(C) 工作壓力。　　　(D) 不好的天氣。

提示：throw up 意為「嘔吐」。

Test **3**

第一部分　看圖辨義

第二部分　問　答

第三部分　簡短對話

腳本與解析

此部分有 15 題，每題都有一張與該題目相對應的圖畫。請聽錄音機播出題目以及 A、B、C、D 四個英語敘述之後，選出與所看到的圖畫最相符的答案。每題只播出一遍。

1

2

3

4 _____

5 _____

6 _____

7 _____

Boarding Pass

Name: Ivan Carter

Flight No.: BA263
Boarding Time: 6:00 PM
Gate: 3 / Seat: 25A

8 _____

9 _____

10 _____

11 _____

12 _____

13 _____

14 _____

15 _____

Track #08

此部分有 15 題，每題請聽錄音機播出一個英語句子之後，從 A、B、C、D 四個回答或回應中，選出一個最適合者作答。每題只播出一遍。

_____ 16 (A) Thank you for the ice cream.

(B) Really? Let's go and have some!

(C) Would it be Japanese or Thai?

(D) Yes. One strawberry, please.

_____ 17 (A) There'll be a game on Friday night.

(B) Thanks for sharing your pictures with me.

(C) How about joining a photography club?

(D) Are you a member of the photography club?

_____ 18 (A) I like rock music best.

(B) Marvelous. I had a great time.

(C) I envy you. When did you go there?

(D) Me too. When would you like to go?

_____ 19 (A) Of course. My friend has just arrived.

(B) Yes. I have two bags to check in.

(C) Sure. Here you are.

(D) Yes. I'd like an aisle seat.

_____ 20 (A) I'll check to see if it's been borrowed.

(B) The library will be closing in half an hour.

(C) You'll need a ladder to get it down.

(D) No problem. Please give me your library card.

_____ 21 (A) I think I'll pass this time.

(B) The ambulance is on its away.

(C) Take your time.

(D) Sure, anytime.

_____ 22 (A) The museum is open from 10 a.m. to 5 p.m.

(B) No, smoking is not allowed here.

(C) Of course. But no flash, please.

(D) I'm sorry. I'll put my camera away.

23 (A) Aren't you hungry?

(B) Do you take credit cards?

(C) It tastes just fine.

(D) OK, if you insist.

24 (A) I'm glad to hear that.

(B) I think we're lost.

(C) Don't panic. Where did you last see it?

(D) May I borrow your camera?

25 (A) I'm traveling alone.

(B) Two weeks.

(C) Here's my passport.

(D) I'm here for sightseeing.

26 (A) He's fifty years old.

(B) He works at a bank.

(C) He's outside, waiting for me.

(D) He's not home right now.

27 (A) Sorry. We're fully booked.

(B) Yes, I'd like to book a flight.

(C) No, there's no message for you, sir.

(D) Yes, I'd like to reserve a room.

28 (A) Sure. There's a demonstration in front of the city hall.

(B) Are you sure? I don't think there's something wrong with my car.

(C) Don't worry. The bus is on schedule.

(D) No problem. You'll get there in time.

29 (A) Housekeeping. May I help you?

(B) Sorry, you have to check out now.

(C) Sure. What else do you need, sir?

(D) Yes, you have two messages, ma'am.

30 (A) That's OK. There's no hurry.

(B) I'd like to buy ten stamps, please.

(C) That'll be US$1.50.

(D) At least three weeks.

Track #09

此部分有 15 題，每題請聽錄音機播出一段對話及一個相關的問題，然後從 A、B、C、D 四個選項中挑出一個最適合的答案。每題只播出一遍。

_____ 31 (A) Her dog is sick.
   (B) Her dog is missing.
   (C) Her dog bit someone.
   (D) Her dog died today.

_____ 32 (A) Quit smoking.
   (B) Put out her cigarette.
   (C) Drink her coffee outside the café.
   (D) Go to another café with better coffee.

_____ 33 (A) The woman's visa for Taiwan.
   (B) The woman's customs declaration.
   (C) His passport.
   (D) His visa for Taiwan.

_____ 34 (A) $5,020.   (B) $5,000.
   (C) $4,020.   (D) $4,000.

35 (A) A big wave is coming.

(B) The sea water is not clean.

(C) The sharks have left.

(D) There are sharks nearby.

36 (A) One o'clock in the afternoon.

(B) Two o'clock in the afternoon.

(C) Four o'clock in the afternoon.

(D) Five o'clock in the afternoon.

37 (A) Buying her a new car.

(B) Having his car fixed.

(C) Buying a second-hand car.

(D) Selling his car.

38 (A) Her co-workers are unfriendly to her.

(B) Her office is too far from her place.

(C) Her pay is too low.

(D) Her apartment is not a nice one.

39 (A) February 1st.

(B) February 3rd.

(C) February 4th.

(D) February 7th.

40 (A) She doesn't know what to write about Taiwan.

(B) She can't hand in her report on time.

(C) She doesn't find writing interesting.

(D) She can't find information about Taiwan's temples.

41 (A) Traveling to southern France.

(B) Studying a second foreign language.

(C) The woman's experience of learning French.

(D) The man's review of the book.

42 (A) She has been to Canada before.

(B) She doesn't want to see snow.

(C) Her travel plans have been canceled.

(D) Canada is too cold in the winter.

43 (A) Fish and coke.

(B) Fish and no drink.

(C) Pork and coke.

(D) Chicken and coke.

44 (A) 12:00 noon.　　(B) 1:00 p.m.

(C) 1:30 p.m.　　(D) 2:00 p.m.

45 (A) The man's letter will be sent to Australia.

(B) The man's package won't be weighed.

(C) The man and the woman are in a restaurant.

(D) The man may send the package by airmail.

1. What are the people running away from?

(A) A house fire.

(B) A forest fire.

(C) A fire in a restaurant.

(D) A fire in a metro station.

問題：這些人在逃離什麼？

選項：(A) 房子失火。

(B) 森林火災。

(C) 餐廳的火災。

(D) 地鐵站的火災。

提示：run away 是「逃走，逃跑」之意。

2. What will the woman hear when the phone is answered?

(A) Room service. What can I do for you?

(B) Housekeeping. May I help you?

(C) Angel Café. Lucy speaking.

(D) Security. How may I help you?

問題：當電話接通時，這個女子會聽到什麼？

選項：(A) 客房服務。我能為您效勞嗎？

(B) 房務部。我能為您服務嗎？

(C) 天使咖啡館。我是 Lucy。

(D) 警衛部門。我能為您效勞嗎？

提示：圖中女子要的是熨斗以及燙衣板，故可知她是
撥電話到飯店的房務部。

---

3. What is the flight attendant saying?

(A) Could you put your bag under the seat in
front of you?

(B) Please go back to your seat immediately.

(C) Could you please store the tray table?

(D) Please fasten your seat belt.

問題：這個空服人員正在說什麼？

選項：(A) 能請您將袋子放到前座的下面嗎？

(B) 麻煩您馬上回到您的座位。

(C) 請您將桌子收起來好嗎？

(D) 請繫上安全帶。

提示：store 在此當動詞用，作「收起」解。

---

4. Where are the people?

(A) At a theater.　　　　(B) On a bus.

(C) At a café.　　　　　(D) In a restaurant.

問題：這些人在哪裡？

選項：(A) 在劇院。　　　　(B) 在公車上。

(C) 在咖啡館裡。　　　(D) 在餐廳裡。

5. Which is true?

(A) The man is taking some medicine.

(B) The patient is feeling much better.

(C) The nurse is taking the patient's temperature.

(D) The patient is seriously ill.

問題：何者屬實？

選項：(A) 男子正在服用藥物。

(B) 病患感覺身體好多了。

(C) 護士正在幫病患量體溫。

(D) 病患病得很嚴重。

提示：take one's temperature 為「量體溫」之意。

---

6. What is the woman saying to the man?

(A) Let me treat you to dinner.

(B) I'd prefer we go Dutch.

(C) That'll be great. Thanks.

(D) What do you want to eat?

問題：這個女子正對男子說些什麼？

選項：(A) 讓我請你吃晚餐。

(B) 我比較想要各付各的帳。

(C) 那太好了。謝謝。

(D) 你想要吃什麼？

7. Which boarding gate will Mr. Carter go to?

(A) 3.　　　　(B) A.　　　　(C) 263.　　　　(D) 25.

問題：Carter 先生會在哪個登機門登機？

選項：(A) 登機門 3。　　　(B) 登機門 A。

(C) 登機門 263。　　(D) 登機門 25。

8. What does the woman want?

(A) Some postcards.　　(B) Some stamps.

(C) Some envelopes.　　(D) Some pictures.

問題：這個女子想要什麼？

選項：(A) 一些明信片。　　(B) 一些郵票。

(C) 一些信封。　　　(D) 一些圖片。

9. What does the man do?

(A) He is a banker.　　(B) He is a police officer.

(C) He is a professor.　　(D) He is a magician.

問題：這個男子是做什麼的？

選項：(A) 他是銀行家。　　(B) 他是警察。

(C) 他是教授。　　　(D) 他是魔術師。

10. What does the man want the woman to do?

(A) Give him a seat near the entrance.

(B) Break the bill into different face values.

(C) Help him make a deposit.

(D) Teach him how to fill out a form.

問題：這個男子要女子做什麼？

選項：(A) 給他一個靠近入口的座位。

(B) 將鈔票換成不同的面額。

(C) 幫他存一筆款項。

(D) 教他如何填寫表格。

提示：make a deposit 為「存款」之意。

---

11. What is the boy not allowed to do?

(A) Swim in the river.

(B) Swim alone in the river.

(C) Fish in the river.

(D) Throw garbage into the river.

問題：這個男孩不被允許做什麼？

選項：(A) 在河裡游泳。

(B) 單獨在河裡游泳。

(C) 在河裡釣魚。

(D) 往河裡丟垃圾。

---

12. What do you think the woman is asking the man?

(A) When will you be arriving?

(B) May I have your boarding pass?

(C) What would you like for breakfast?

(D) Do you have a reservation?

問題：你覺得這個女子正在問男子什麼？

選項：(A) 您將在何時抵達呢？

(B) 可以給我您的登機證嗎？

(C) 您早餐想吃什麼？

(D) 您有預約嗎？

---

13. What does the girl want to do?

(A) Borrow some books.

(B) Return some books.

(C) Buy some books from the man.

(D) Sell some books to the man.

問題：這個女孩想要做什麼？

選項：(A) 借一些書。

(B) 還一些書。

(C) 從男子那買一些書。

(D) 賣給男子一些書。

---

14. What are they talking about?

(A) Transportation.   (B) Traffic.

(C) Weather.   (D) Food.

問題：他們在討論什麼？

選項：(A) 交通工具。　　(B) 交通。

　　　(C) 天氣。　　　　(D) 食物。

- -

15. What does the man want?

(A) A job in the tourist office.

(B) Some newspapers.

(C) Some beautiful photos of Taroko Gorge.

(D) Some information about Taroko Gorge.

問題：這個男子想要什麼？

選項：(A) 一份在遊客中心的工作。

　　　(B) 一些報紙。

　　　(C) 一些美麗的太魯閣照片。

　　　(D) 一些關於太魯閣的資訊。

第二部分　腳本與解析　 Track #08

16. Do you like ice cream? I know a perfect place nearby.

(A) Thank you for the ice cream.

(B) Really? Let's go and have some!

(C) Would it be Japanese or Thai?

(D) Yes. One strawberry, please.

問題：你喜歡吃冰淇淋嗎？我知道附近有一個很棒的
　　　地方。

選項：(A) 謝謝你請我吃冰淇淋。

　　　(B) 真的嗎？我們一起去吃一些吧！

　　　(C) 它是日式的還是泰式的？

　　　(D) 是的。請給我一球草莓口味的。

提示：Thai 在此為形容詞，表「泰國的」。

---

17. I wish I knew how to take good pictures.

(A) There'll be a game on Friday night.

(B) Thanks for sharing your pictures with me.

(C) How about joining a photography club?

(D) Are you a member of the photography club?

問題：我真希望我知道怎麼拍出好照片。

選項：(A) 星期五晚上將有一場比賽。

　　　(B) 謝謝你跟我分享你的照片。

　　　(C) 加入攝影社如何？

　　　(D) 你是這個攝影社的社員嗎？

---

18. I've always wanted to visit Salzburg, Mozart's
hometown.

(A) I like rock music best.

(B) Marvelous. I had a great time.

(C) I envy you. When did you go there?

(D) Me too. When would you like to go?

問題：我一直很想去莫札特的家鄉薩爾斯堡。

選項：(A) 我最喜歡搖滾樂。

　　　(B) 太棒了。我玩得很開心。

　　　(C) 我真羨慕你。你何時去的？

　　　(D) 我也是。你想要什麼時候去？

---

19. May I have your passport, please?

(A) Of course. My friend has just arrived.

(D) Yes. I have two bags to check in.

(C) Sure. Here you are.

(D) Yes. I'd like an aisle seat.

問題：麻煩請給我你的護照好嗎？

選項：(A) 當然。我的朋友剛抵達。

　　　(B) 是的。我有兩個袋子要辦理託運。

　　　(C) 好的。拿去吧。

　　　(D) 是的。我想要靠走道的位子。

提示：aisle 為「走道，走廊」之意。

---

20. The book I'm trying to find isn't on the shelf.

(A) I'll check to see if it's been borrowed.

(B) The library will be closing in half an hour.

(C) You'll need a ladder to get it down.

(D) No problem. Please give me your library

card.

問題：我在找的書不在書架上。

選項：(A) 我來看看它是否已被借走了。

(B) 圖書館在半小時內即將關館。

(C) 你會需要梯子把它拿下來。

(D) 沒問題。請給我你的借書證。

---

21. My sister's just fallen downstairs, and she is in great pain.

(A) I think I'll pass this time.

(B) The ambulance is on its away.

(C) Take your time.

(D) Sure, anytime.

問題：我姊姊剛才摔下樓梯，她現在非常痛。

選項：(A) 我想這次我就算了。

(B) 救護車在路上了。

(C) 慢慢來，不急。

(D) 當然，隨時都可以。

---

22. Excuse me, are we allowed to take photos in the museum?

(A) The museum is open from 10 a.m. to 5 p.m.

(B) No, smoking is not allowed here.

(C) Of course. But no flash, please.

(D) I'm sorry. I'll put my camera away.

問題：不好意思，我們可以在博物館裡拍照嗎？

選項：(A) 博物館開館時間為上午十點到下午五點。

　　　(B) 不行，這裡不能抽菸。

　　　(C) 當然。但請勿使用閃光燈。

　　　(D) 對不起。我會把相機收起來。

提示：put...away 在此表「收起……」。

---

23. You treated me to lunch last time, so this meal is on me.

(A) Aren't you hungry?

(B) Do you take credit cards?

(C) It tastes just fine.

(D) OK, if you insist.

問題：你上次請我吃午餐，所以這餐算我的。

選項：(A) 你不餓嗎？

　　　(B) 你們收信用卡嗎？

　　　(C) 它嚐起來還可以。

　　　(D) 如果你堅持的話，好吧。

提示：treat sb to... 作「招待某人……」解。

---

24. Oh, no! I think I lost my camera.

(A) I'm glad to hear that.

(B) I think we're lost.

(C) Don't panic. Where did you last see it?

(D) May I borrow your camera?

問題：噢，不！我想我的相機不見了。

選項：(A) 我很高興聽到這件事。

　　　(B) 我想我們迷路了

　　　(C) 別慌張。你最後一次在哪裡看到它？

　　　(D) 我可以跟你借相機嗎？

---

25. What's the purpose of your visit?

(A) I'm traveling alone.

(B) Two weeks.

(C) Here's my passport.

(D) I'm here for sightseeing.

問題：你的參訪目的是什麼？

選項：(A) 我獨自旅行。

　　　(B) 兩個星期。

　　　(C) 這是我的護照。

　　　(D) 我來這兒觀光。

---

26. What does your father do?

(A) He's fifty years old.

(B) He works at a bank.

(C) He's outside, waiting for me.

(D) He's not home right now.

問題：你父親是做什麼的？

選項：(A) 他五十歲了。

(B) 他在一家銀行工作。

(C) 他在外面等著我。

(D) 他現在不在家。

---

27. Good morning, Fairy Hotel. May I help you?

(A) Sorry. We're fully booked.

(B) Yes, I'd like to book a flight.

(C) No, there's no message for you, sir.

(D) Yes, I'd like to reserve a room.

問題：早安，Fairy 飯店。我能為您服務嗎？

選項：(A) 抱歉。我們客滿了。

(B) 是的，我想要訂張機票。

(C) 不，先生，沒有任何人留言給您。

(D) 是的，我想要預訂房間。

---

28. Excuse me. Could you tell me why the traffic is moving so slowly today?

(A) Sure. There's a demonstration in front of the city hall.

(B) Are you sure? I don't think there's something wrong with my car.

(C) Don't worry. The bus is on schedule.

(D) No problem. You'll get there in time.

問題：不好意思。你能告訴我今天路上的車輛為何移動得這麼慢嗎？

選項：(A) 當然。因為在市政府前面有一場示威活動。

(B) 你確定嗎？我覺得我的車子沒有問題。

(C) 別擔心。這班公車很準時。

(D) 沒問題。你會及時到那兒的。

提示：on schedule 為「按照預定時間」之意，即「準時」，on time 亦表「準時」，而 in time 則表示「及時」。

---

29. Excuse me. Could you send a cheeseburger and an iced tea to my room?

(A) Housekeeping. May I help you?

(B) Sorry, you have to check out now.

(C) Sure. What else do you need, sir?

(D) Yes, you have two messages, ma'am.

問題：不好意思。你可以送一個起司漢堡和一杯冰茶到我房間嗎？

選項：(A) 房務部。我能為您服務嗎？

(B) 抱歉，您必須現在退房。

(C) 當然。先生，您還需要些別的嗎？

(D) 是的，女士，您有兩則留言。

30. Surface mail is the cheapest, but it is really slow.

(A) That's OK. There's no hurry.

(B) I'd like to buy ten stamps, please.

(C) That'll be US$1.50.

(D) At least three weeks.

問題：平信最便宜，但真的很慢。

選項：(A) 沒關係。不趕時間。

(B) 我要買十張郵票，麻煩你。

(C) 總共是一點五美元。

(D) 至少要三個星期。

<hr>

第三部分　腳本與解析　 Track #09

31. M: Have you found Coach?

W: No. I've tried everywhere, but I just can't find him. I think someone must have taken him.

M: Don't be discouraged. I'll help you look for him after work today.

W: Thanks. Coach is a really nice dog. I just can't imagine what my life will be like without him.

Q: Why is the woman upset?

(A) Her dog is sick.

(B) Her dog is missing.

(C) Her dog bit someone.

(D) Her dog died today.

男：你找到 Coach 了嗎？

女：沒有。我每個地方都找過了，但就是找不到牠。我想牠一定被某人帶走了。

男：別沮喪。我今天下班後會再幫你找。

女：謝謝。Coach 真的是一隻很棒的狗。我真不能想像沒有牠在我身邊的日子會是怎樣。

問題：這個女子為何難過？

選項：(A) 她的狗生病了。

(B) 她的狗不見了。

(C) 她的狗咬了別人。

(D) 她的狗今天死了。

---

32. W: Excuse me. Is it OK to smoke in the café?

M: I'm sorry. You can't smoke in here, but you can smoke outside.

W: Oh, thanks. Would you bring my coffee outside?

M: No problem.

Q: What is the woman going to do?

(A) Quit smoking.

(B) Put out her cigarette.

(C) Drink her coffee outside the café.

(D) Go to another café with better coffee.

女：不好意思，這咖啡館裡可以抽菸嗎？

男：很抱歉。你不可以在裡面抽菸，但你可以在外面抽。

女：哦，謝謝。你能把我的咖啡拿到外面嗎？

男：沒問題。

問題．這個女子接下來會做什麼？

選項：(A) 戒菸。

　　　(B) 熄掉她的菸。

　　　(C) 在咖啡館外面喝咖啡。

　　　(D) 去另一家咖啡比較好喝的咖啡館。

提示：put out 為「熄滅」之意。

---

33. M: I don't see your visa for Taiwan.

W: It should be in there. May I show it to you?

M: Please.

W: Let me see. Here. It's on page 25. I have too many visas in my passport.

Q: What was the man unable to find?

(A) The woman's visa for Taiwan.

(B) The woman's customs declaration.

(C) His passport.

(D) His visa for Taiwan.

男：我沒有看到你的臺灣簽證。

女：應該在裡面。我可以翻給你看嗎？

男：麻煩你了。

女：讓我看看。在這裡。在第二十五頁。我的護照裡
　　有太多簽證了。

問題：這個男子找不到什麼東西？

選項：(A) 女子的臺灣簽證。

　　　(B) 女子的海關申報表。

　　　(C) 他的護照。

　　　(D) 他的臺灣簽證。

提示：customs 為「海關」之意，customs
　　　declaration 則是「海關申報表」。

- -

34. W: How much is the bill?

M: $5,000, service charge included.

W: Let me pay for it. I'm a member of this club,
and I can get a 20% discount.

M: OK. But let's make a deal that I'll pay for
your meal next time.

Q: How much will the woman pay?

(A) $5,020.　　　　　　(B) $5,000.

(C) $4,020.　　　　　　(D) $4,000.

女：帳單是多少錢？

男：五千元，含服務費。

女：這次讓我付錢吧。我是這個俱樂部的會員，我可以有百分之二十的折扣。

男：好。不過我們打個商量，下次讓我幫你付餐錢。

問題：這個女子將付多少錢？

選項：(A) 5,020 元。　　(B) 5,000 元。
　　　(C) 4,020 元。　　(D) 4,000 元。

提示：有百分之二十的折扣，等同於八折，五千元打八折，故女子要付四千元。

---

35. M: Do you see what I see?

W: Yes. There are at least two sharks out there.

M: I'll turn on the alarm so the swimmers will come back to shore.

W: OK. I'll keep an eye on the sharks.

Q: What would the alarm tell the swimmers?

(A) A big wave is coming.

(B) The sea water is not clean.

(C) The sharks have left.

(D) There are sharks nearby.

男：你有看到我看到的東西嗎？

女：有。那裡至少有兩隻鯊魚。

男：我去將警鈴打開，這樣子游泳的人會回到岸邊

來。

女：好。我會注意著那些鯊魚。

問題：警鈴會告知游泳的人什麼？

選項：(A) 有大浪要來了。

　　　(B) 海水不乾淨。

　　　(C) 鯊魚離開了。

　　　(D) 附近有鯊魚。

提示：keep an eye on sth 表「留意……」。

---

36. W: Is there a library sale today?

M: Yes. It'll begin at 2:00 p.m. in the reading room on the 4th floor.

W: Thanks. Could you tell me about the prices?

M: It's $100 for a hardcover and $50 for a paperback.

Q: When will the library sale begin?

(A) One o'clock in the afternoon.

(B) Two o'clock in the afternoon.

(C) Four o'clock in the afternoon.

(D) Five o'clock in the afternoon.

女：今天有圖書特賣會嗎？

男：有的。特賣會於下午兩點在四樓的閱覽室開始。

女：謝謝。你能跟我說一下價格嗎？

男：精裝本一本一百元，平裝本一本五十元。

問題：圖書館特賣會何時開始？

選項：(A) 下午一點。　　(B) 下午兩點。

　　　(C) 下午四點。　　(D) 下午五點。

提示：hardcover 為「精裝本，硬皮書」；paperback
　　　為「平裝本，平裝書」。

- -

37. M: Oh, no. I can't start the car again. It's the
third time this week.

W: How long have you had this car?

M: Almost ten years.

W: Maybe you should buy a new one.

M: But I can't afford a new car. New cars are too
expensive.

W: How about a second-hand car?

Q: What did the woman suggest to the man?

(A) Buying her a new car.

(B) Having his car fixed.

(C) Buying a second-hand car.

(D) Selling his car.

男：哦，不。車子又發不動了。是這星期第三次了。

女：你這臺車多久了？

男：快十年了。

女：或許你該買臺新的了。

男：可是我買不起一輛新車。新車太貴了。

女：那麼二手車呢？

問題：這個女子對男子建議什麼？

選項：(A) 買一臺新車給她。

(B) 將他的車送修。

(C) 買一輛二手車。

(D) 賣掉他的車。

---

38. M: I think you should hang on to your job. It's the best one you've ever had.

W: I know, but it's really far from where I live.

M: But the pay is good and your co-workers are nice. Why don't you find an apartment closer to your office?

W: That's a good idea. How come I didn't think of that?

Q: What is the woman's problem?

(A) Her co-workers are unfriendly to her.

(B) Her office is too far from her place.

(C) Her pay is too low.

(D) Her apartment is not a nice one.

男：我覺得你應該好好把握這份工作。它是你有過最好的工作了。

女：我知道，可是它真的離我住的地方好遠。

男：可是薪水很不錯，你的同事也都很好。你何不找

離你辦公室較近的公寓住呢？

女：這主意不錯。我怎麼會沒想到呢？

問題：這個女子的問題是什麼？

選項：(A) 她的同事對她不友善。

　　　(B) 她的辦公室離家太遠。

　　　(C) 她的薪水太低。

　　　(D) 她的公寓不是很好。

提示：hang on 意為「緊抓住」，在此作「把握」解；
　　　how come...? 表示「怎麼會……？」之意。

---

39. M: Hello, I'd like to book four seats on the flight to Bali on February 1st, please.

W: Just a moment. I'm sorry, sir. There won't be any seats until the 3rd.

M: The 3rd will be fine.

W: OK. When would you like to come back?

M: On the 7th.

Q: When will the man leave for Bali?

(A) February 1st.　　　　(B) February 3rd.

(C) February 4th.　　　　(D) February 7th.

男：你好，我想要預訂四個二月一號到巴里島的機位。

女：請稍候。很抱歉，先生。要到三號才有機位。

男：三號也沒關係。

女：好的。請問您想哪一天回來？

男：當月七號。

問題：這個男子何時會出發到巴里島？

選項：(A) 二月一日。　　(B) 二月三日。

　　　(C) 二月四日。　　(D) 二月七日。

....

40. W: I need your opinion on something I'm working on.

M: Sure. What is it?

W: I'm writing a report about Taiwan, but there're too many topics and I don't know which topic to choose.

M: Why don't you talk about Taiwan's temples? I think it'll be interesting.

Q: What is the woman's problem?

(A) She doesn't know what to write about Taiwan.

(B) She can't hand in her report on time.

(C) She doesn't find writing interesting.

(D) She can't find information about Taiwan's temples.

女：有關我現在在做的事，我需要你的意見。

男：沒問題。是什麼呢？

女：我正在寫一篇有關臺灣的報告，但是有好多主

題，而我不知道該選哪一個。

男：你何不介紹臺灣的廟宇？我想會很有趣。

問題：這個女子的問題是什麼？

選項：(A) 她不知道要寫臺灣的什麼。

　　　(B) 她無法準時繳交報告。

　　　(C) 她不覺得寫作有趣。

　　　(D) 她找不到有關臺灣廟宇的資訊。

提示：find 除了有「找到」的意思外，還可表示「發覺」之意，即選項(C)中的意思。

- -

41. M: If you have a chance, would you study another foreign language besides English?

W: Yes, I would. I'd like to study French.

M: May I ask why?

W: Ever since I read the book *A Year in Provence*, I became interested in France. I hope some day I'll be able to travel to southern France.

Q: What are they talking about?

(A) Traveling to southern France.

(B) Studying a second foreign language.

(C) The woman's experience of learning French.

(D) The man's review of the book.

男：如果有機會，除了英語，你會學另一種外語嗎？

女：我會。我想要學法文。

男：我可以請問為什麼嗎？

女：自從我讀了《山居歲月——普羅旺斯的一年》之後，我對法國就很有興趣。我希望有一天我能去法國南部旅行。

問題：他們在談論什麼？

選項：(A) 旅行到法國南部。

(B) 學習第二種外國語言。

(C) 女子學法文的經驗。

(D) 男子對那本書的評論。

---

42. M: What do you say we go to Canada for our holidays?

W: In the winter? It'll be freezing!

M: Don't you think it'll be fun to see the snow? I've never seen snow before.

W: True. But think about snowstorms. Our travel plans might be canceled by all kinds of delays.

Q: Why does the woman oppose the man's idea?

(A) She has been to Canada before.

(B) She doesn't want to see snow.

(C) Her travel plans have been canceled.

(D) Canada is too cold in the winter.

男：你覺得我們去加拿大渡假如何？

女：在冬天去？會很冷耶！

男：你不覺得可以看到雪很好玩嗎？我以前從沒看過雪。

女：是啦。可是想想暴風雪。我們的旅行計畫可能會因為各式各樣的延誤而取消。

問題：這個女子為何反對男子的想法？

選項：(A) 她已經去過加拿大。

(B) 她不想看雪。

(C) 她的旅行計畫已取消。

(D) 加拿大的冬天太冷。

提示：freezing 意為「極冷的」。

---

43. W: Good evening. Would you like to have chicken, fish, or pork for dinner?

M: Fish, please.

W: Anything to drink?

M: Yes. A coke, please.

Q: What did the man want for dinner?

(A) Fish and coke.

(B) Fish and no drink.

(C) Pork and coke.

(D) Chicken and coke.

女：晚安。請問您晚餐要吃雞肉、魚肉或豬肉？

男：魚肉，麻煩你。

女：要喝什麼飲料嗎？

男：好啊。麻煩一杯可樂。

問題：這個男子要什麼當晚餐？

選項：(A) 魚和可樂。

　　　(B) 魚，沒有飲料。

　　　(C) 豬肉和可樂。

　　　(D) 雞肉和可樂。

---

44. W: Here's your room key, and the elevator is in the corner.

M: Thank you. By the way, when is the check-out time?

W: Twelve noon.

M: Would it be possible to give me one extra hour? I don't think I'll be able to make it back before tomorrow noon.

W: No problem. Enjoy your stay.

Q: When will the man be checking out tomorrow?

(A) 12:00 noon.　　　(B) 1:00 p.m.

(C) 1:30 p.m.　　　(D) 2:00 p.m.

女：這是您的房間鑰匙，電梯就在角落那兒。

男：謝謝你。對了，請問退房時間是什麼時候？

女：中午十二點。

男：請問有可能多給我一小時嗎？我想我明天中午前大概還回不來。

女：沒問題。祝您住宿愉快。

問題：這個男子明天幾點會退房？

選項：(A) 中午十二點。　(B) 下午一點。

　　　(C) 下午一點半。　(D) 下午兩點。

提示：by the way 表示「順便一提」。

---

45. M: Hi, I'd like to send this package to Australia and this letter to the U.S.

W: Sure. How would you like to send the package?

M: How much will it be if I send it by airmail?

W: It depends on what's inside the package and its weight.

Q: Which is true?

(A) The man's letter will be sent to Australia.

(B) The man's package won't be weighed.

(C) The man and the woman are in a restaurant.

(D) The man may send the package by airmail.

男：你好。我要寄這個包裹到澳洲，這封信則要寄到美國。

女：好的。請問您想怎麼寄這個包裹？

男：如果以航空郵件寄送需要多少郵資？

女：那要看包裹裡面是什麼東西以及它的重量而定。

問題：何者屬實？

選項：(A) 男子的信會被寄到澳洲。

　　　(B) 男子的包裹將不會被秤重。

　　　(C) 男子可能以航空郵件寄出包裹。

　　　(D) 這個男子跟女子是在餐廳裡。

提示：A depend on B 為「A 視 B 的情況而定」。

第一部分　看圖辨義

Track #10

此部分有 15 題，每題都有一張與該題目相對應的圖畫。請聽錄音機播出題目以及 A、B、C、D 四個英語敘述之後，選出與所看到的圖畫最相符的答案。每題只播出一遍。

1

2

3

全民英檢聽力通 126

4 _____

5 _____

6 _____

7 _____

8 _____

9 _____

10 _____

11 _____

此部分有 15 題，每題請聽錄音機播出一個英語句子之後，從 A、B、C、D 四個回答或回應中，選出一個最適合者作答。每題只播出一遍。

16 (A) Maple and First Streets.

　(B) It's 3:00 p.m.

　(C) Half an hour ago.

　(D) The car bumped into a tree.

17 (A) I don't know. What do you think?

　(B) You're right. Baseball drives me crazy.

　(C) I'm sorry. I have other plans for tonight.

　(D) Yeah. I wouldn't miss any baseball games.

18 (A) I'm glad you like them.

　(B) Thank you. These flowers are beautiful.

　(C) I'm really sorry. Thanks for warning me.

(D) I'm sure you will love those flowers.

19 (A) OK. Sounds great.

(B) Thanks for your help.

(C) Sorry. I need my computer today.

(D) Sure. Let me take a look at it.

20 (A) Special delivery. It'll get there in 24 hours.

(B) Airmail costs more than surface mail.

(C) How would you like to send it?

(D) That'll be $350.

21 (A) How do you like the Science Club?

(B) No problem. I love the Book Club.

(C) Yes. I'm going to sign up for it tomorrow.

(D) You should come along next week.

22 (A) The restaurant opens at 11:00 a.m.

(B) There's a night market two blocks away.

(C) You can use the washing machine anytime.

(D) Sure. Your room number, please.

23 (A) Sure. January is fine with me.

(B) Is that so? I think Italy is fantastic.

(C) What? I thought you wanted to go to Italy.

(D) Great. I've always wanted to see that country.

24 (A) Yes. It's $120 for one way.

(B) Yes. It stops at several major hotels.

(C) Yes. It runs every 20 minutes.

(D) Yes. Go straight and turn left. You won't miss it.

25 (A) Wow, she must like you very much!

(B) Gee, I'm sorry to hear that.

(C) Really? Is your boss interesting?

(D) Congratulations. I'm happy for you.

26 (A) Just take the elevator over there to the 2nd floor.

(B) Gate 18 is at Terminal 1, not Terminal 2.

(C) Yes. You'll be boarding at Gate 18.

(D) Your boarding time is 8:30 p.m.

27 (A) Here is your boarding pass.

(B) Yes. I'd like to have some tea, please.

(C) Could you tell me when we'll be boarding?

(D) Hi. Could you show me where seat 34C is?

28 (A) Yes, it's a great movie.

(B) Cool! Let's go see it.

(C) Sorry, I don't watch romantic movies.

(D) Sure! Science fiction is my favorite.

29 (A) Yes. I'll have one beef sandwich and a milk.

(B) Yes. I'd like a single room, please.

(C) Yes. I called six days ago to reserve a room for tonight.

(D) Yes. I'd like to have this skirt washed and ironed.

30 (A) He is leaving for Germany tomorrow.

(B) He likes his first company best.

(C) He is not easy to get along with.

(D) He's never talked about it.

此部分有 15 題，每題請聽錄音機播出一段對話及一個相關的問題，然後從 A、B、C、D 四個選項中挑出一個最適合的答案。每題只播出一遍。

_____ 31 (A) Booking a seat on a flight.
　　　(B) Canceling all of his reservations.
　　　(C) Leaving a message to a hotel guest.
　　　(D) Changing the date of his reservation.

_____ 32 (A) In a fire department.
　　　(B) In a grocery store.
　　　(C) In a museum.
　　　(D) In a school.

_____ 33 (A) He wants to close the overhead compartment.
　　　(B) He wants a place to put his bag.
　　　(C) He wants his bag to go under his seat.
　　　(D) He wants to empty his bag.

_____ 34 (A) Letters.   (B) Catalogs.
      (C) Magazines.   (D) Books.

_____ 35 (A) In 50-pound bills.
      (B) In 20-pound bills.
      (C) In 10-pound bills.
      (D) In 5-pound bills.

_____ 36 (A) The woman is a doctor.
      (B) The baby got hurt.
      (C) The man will examine the baby.
      (D) They are in a fire station.

_____ 37 (A) Ask the woman to pay him money.
      (B) Ask the library to buy a book for him.
      (C) Return his library card to the library.
      (D) Buy a copy of _The Handbook of Joy_.

_____ 38 (A) The beginning.
      (B) The story.
      (C) The music.
      (D) The ending.

39 (A) Trying some sweets.

(B) Giving her some chocolate.

(C) Going to a doctor.

(D) Stopping eating chocolate.

40 (A) She reminded him to see a doctor.

(B) She told him the same thing had happened to her.

(C) She would introduce her friend to him.

(D) She would take a week's vacation with him.

41 (A) How to treat each other.

(B) Where to have dinner.

(C) Who was to pay the bill.

(D) Who was to be invited for dinner.

42 (A) The girl's parents were sick.

(B) The boy's swimming club won first prize.

(C) The swimming club changed their coach.

(D) The girl went to see the swimming contest.

43 (A) The man will go to South Africa with the woman.
(B) The man is interested in visiting South Africa.
(C) The woman is interested in wild animals.
(D) The woman has been to South Africa.

44 (A) The store where he bought the TV.
(B) The cable TV operator.
(C) The TV manufacturer.
(D) The TV station.

45 (A) 500 dollars.　(B) 2,000 dollars.
(C) 1,500 dollars.　(D) 1,000 dollars.

1. What is the man's problem?

(A) His car was hit by another car.

(B) He was stopped for speeding.

(C) He has a flat tire.

(D) His car was stolen.

問題：這個男子的問題是什麼？

選項：(A) 他的車子被另一部車子撞了。

　　　(B) 他因為超速而被攔下了。

　　　(C) 他的車子輪胎漏氣了。

　　　(D) 他的車子被偷了。

提示：flat tire 表示「輪胎漏氣」之意。

2. What is the man saying to the woman?

(A) May I see your ID?

(B) How may I help you?

(C) You can't trespass on the lawn.

(D) You are free to go through.

問題：這個男子對女子說什麼？

選項：(A) 可以給我看你的身分證嗎？

　　　(B) 我能為你服務嗎？

　　　(C) 你不能穿越這草坪。

(D) 你可以過去了。

提示：trespass 為「擅自進入，闖入」之意。圖中標誌的 "No Trespassing" 意為「禁止擅自進入」，"Private Property" 則表示「私人財產」。

---

3. What does the man want to be sure of?
   (A) Whether the woman will bring him the check.
   (B) Whether he needs to bring any warm clothes.
   (C) Whether the price has included breakfast.
   (D) Whether his room reservation is OK.

   問題：這個男子想要確定什麼？
   選項：(A) 女子是否會拿帳單給他。
   　　　(B) 他是否需要帶厚重衣物。
   　　　(C) 價格是否已包含早餐。
   　　　(D) 他的訂房是否沒問題。

---

4. What is the girl doing?
   (A) Waiting for the meal she ordered.
   (B) Waiting to check in her baggage.
   (C) Waiting to board a plane.
   (D) Waiting for her baggage.

   問題：這個女孩正在做什麼？

選項：(A) 等她點的餐點。

　　　(B) 等著託運行李。

　　　(C) 等著登機。

　　　(D) 等著領行李。

提示：「領行李」可以用 claim baggage 表示。

- -

5. What is wrong with the woman?

(A) She has a fever.

(B) She injured her back.

(C) She has a stomachache.

(D) She broke her arm.

問題：這個女子怎麼了？

選項：(A) 她發燒了。　　　(B) 她的背受傷了。

　　　(C) 她胃痛。　　　(D) 她的手臂斷了。

- -

6. What kind of book is the man trying to find?

(A) A work of classic fiction.

(B) A collection of poetry.

(C) A book about European history.

(D) A book about using a camera.

問題：這個男子想要找什麼樣的書？

選項：(A) 一本經典小説。

　　　(B) 一本詩集。

　　　(C) 一本談論歐洲歷史的書。

(D) 一本談論相機使用的書。

提示：由圖中的 "Photography" 一字可得知這個男
子是站在與攝影相關的書籍前面，故可推論他
想要找的書與攝影有關。

---

7. What would the man say to the woman?

(A) Hello. May I help you?

(B) What's your service charge?

(C) Please send these postcards by airmail.

(D) I'd like to check out this book, please.

問題：這個男子會對女子說什麼？

選項：(A) 您好，我能為您效勞嗎？

(B) 請問你們的手續費是多少？

(C) 請用航空郵遞寄送這些明信片。

(D) 麻煩你，我要借這本書。

提示：選項(A)應該是女子會說的話，而選項(C)和(D)則
不符合此圖。

---

8. Where is the woman working?

(A) At a hotel.

(B) At a flower shop.

(C) In a bookstore.

(D) In a department store.

問題：這個女子在哪裡工作？

選項：(A) 在飯店裡。　　(B) 在花店裡。

　　　(C) 在書局裡。　　(D) 在百貨公司裡。

---

9. What is the old lady saying to the flight attendant?

(A) Could you take my bag down from the overhead compartment, please?

(B) Could you please show me where the lavatory is?

(C) Any English newspapers will be fine.

(D) If it's possible, I'd like to change seats.

問題：這個老太太對空服員說了什麼？

選項：(A) 麻煩你將我的包包從上頭的隔層拿下來好嗎？

　　　(B) 麻煩你告訴我洗手間在哪好嗎？

　　　(C) 任何英語的報紙都可以。

　　　(D) 如果可能的話，我想換座位。

提示：compartment 原意表「隔層，隔間」，在此指位於機艙兩邊上方的行李隔層；overhead 則為「頭頂上的」。

---

10. What is the clerk explaining to the guest?

(A) What the hotel rooms look like.

(B) Where the hotel is.

(C) The hotel's room rates.

(D) The hotel's services.

問題：這個職員正在對客人解釋什麼？

選項：(A) 飯店房間的樣子。

(B) 飯店位於何處。

(C) 飯店房間的價格。

(D) 飯店提供的服務。

---

11. What does the woman prefer to do?

(A) Go fishing.

(B) Go to the beach.

(C) Spend time in the mountains.

(D) Stay in a five-star hotel.

問題：這個女子比較喜歡做什麼？

選項：(A) 去釣魚。

(B) 去海邊玩。

(C) 花時間待在山上。

(D) 待在五星級飯店裡。

---

12. What is the man saying to the woman?

(A) Let me take you to the hospital.

(B) What happened to you?

(C) Don't worry. You are a good doctor.

(D) Are you a nurse?

問題：這個男子正對女子説什麼？

選項：(A) 讓我送你去醫院吧。

(B) 你怎麼了？

(C) 別擔心。你是個好醫生。

(D) 你是護士嗎？

---

13. What is the man doing?

(A) Receiving an award.

(B) Taking a listening test.

(C) Having an interview.

(D) Ordering some food.

問題：這個男子正在做什麼？

選項：(A) 接受頒獎。

(B) 參加聽力測驗。

(C) 參加面試。

(D) 點餐。

提示：award 做「獎，獎賞」解。

---

14. What would the man say to the woman?

(A) Thank you very much.

(B) Have a nice trip.

(C) You're welcome.

(D) You'll be boarding at Gate 2.

問題：這個男子會對女子説什麼？

選項：(A) 非常謝謝你。

(B) 旅途愉快。

(C) 不客氣。

(D) 你將在二號登機門登機。

提示：根據圖片，選項(B) 、(C) 、(D)都是女子 (機場地勤人員) 可能會說的話，故選(A)。

---

15. What's wrong with the man?

(A) He is wet because of heavy rain.

(B) He is covered with sweat.

(C) He is angry.

(D) He is very cold.

問題：這個男子怎麼了？

選項：(A) 他因大雨而淋濕了。

(B) 他滿身大汗。

(C) 他在生氣。

(D) 他很冷。

提示：be covered with sweat 表示「滿身大汗」，sweat 在此為名詞，意為「汗水」。

第二部分 腳本與解析

Track #11

16. Where is the accident?

(A) Maple and First Streets.

(B) It's 3:00 p.m.

(C) Half an hour ago.

(D) The car bumped into a tree.

問題：

選項：(A) 楓葉街與第一街。

　　　(B) 下午三點。

　　　(C) 半個小時前。

　　　(D) 那輛車撞到一棵樹。

提示：where 是問地點，故選(A)。

---

17. Is it true that you are crazy about baseball?

(A) I don't know. What do you think?

(B) You're right. Baseball drives me crazy.

(C) I'm sorry. I have other plans for tonight.

(D) Yeah. I wouldn't miss any baseball games.

問題：你很瘋棒球這件事是真的嗎？

選項：(A) 我不知道。你覺得呢？

　　　(B) 沒錯。棒球快把我搞瘋了。

　　　(C) 很抱歉。我今晚有別的計畫了。

　　　(D) 對啊，我不會錯過任何的棒球比賽。

提示：A be crazy about B 是「A 為 B 而瘋狂」，表
　　　示 A 很喜歡 B 的意思；A drive B crazy 卻是
　　　「A 讓 B 抓狂」，表示 B 很不喜歡 A。

18. Excuse me. You're not allowed to pick the flowers. It's against the rules.

(A) I'm glad you like them.

(B) Thank you. These flowers are beautiful.

(C) I'm really sorry. Thanks for warning me.

(D) I'm sure you will love those flowers.

問題：不好意思。你不能摘這些花。那是違反規定的。

選項：(A) 我很高興你喜歡他們。

(B) 謝謝你。這些花很漂亮。

(C) 真是抱歉。謝謝你警告我。

(D) 我相信你會喜歡那些花的。

---

19. My computer is broken down. Could you help me?

(A) OK. Sounds great.

(B) Thanks for your help.

(C) Sorry. I need my computer today.

(D) Sure. Let me take a look at it.

問題：我的電腦壞掉了。你能幫我嗎？

選項：(A) 好啊。聽起來不錯。

(B) 謝謝你的幫忙。

(C) 抱歉。我今天需要我的電腦。

(D) 當然。讓我幫你看看。

提示：break down 表「壞掉」。

20. I'd like to have this package delivered to Chicago as soon as possible. What is the best way to send it?

(A) Special delivery. It'll get there in 24 hours.

(B) Airmail costs more than surface mail.

(C) How would you like to send it?

(D) That'll be $350.

問題：我希望這個包裹可以盡快寄到芝加哥。以哪一種方式寄送它最好？

選項：(A) 特別投遞。它會在 24 小時內抵達。

(B) 航空郵寄比海陸郵寄花較多郵資。

(C) 你想要怎麼寄送？

(D) 總共是 350 元。

21. If you're interested in writing, you should write for our school paper.

(A) How do you like the Science Club?

(B) No problem. I love the Book Club.

(C) Yes. I'm going to sign up for it tomorrow.

(D) You should come along next week.

問題：如果你對寫作有興趣，你應該幫校刊寫東西。

選項：(A) 你覺得科學社如何？

(B) 沒問題。我很喜歡讀書社。

(C) 好。我明天就會去報名。

(D) 你下星期應該一起來。

提示：sign up 為「報名參加，同意從事」之意。

---

22. Excuse me. Do you know where I can get something to eat at this late hour?

(A) The restaurant opens at 11:00 a.m.

(B) There's a night market two blocks away.

(C) You can use the washing machine anytime.

(D) Sure. Your room number, please.

問題：不好意思。你知道這麼晚了我能去哪裡找些東西吃嗎？

選項：(A) 那間餐廳上午 11 點開始營業。

(B) 兩條街外有個夜市。

(C) 你可以在任何時間使用洗衣機。

(D) 沒問題。請給我你的房號。

---

23. What do you say we go to Italy for the holidays?

(A) Sure. January is fine with me.

(B) Is that so? I think Italy is fantastic.

(C) What? I thought you wanted to go to Italy.

(D) Great. I've always wanted to see that

country.

問題：你看我們去義大利渡假如何？

選項：(A) 沒問題。一月我可以。

(B) 是那樣嗎？我覺得義大利很棒啊。

(C) 什麼？我以為你想去義大利呢。

(D) 太好了。我一直想去看看那個國家。

- -

24. Hi, could you tell me how often the airport bus runs?

(A) Yes. It's $120 for one way.

(B) Yes. It stops at several major hotels.

(C) Yes. It runs every 20 minutes.

(D) Yes. Go straight and turn left. You won't miss it.

問題：嗨，你可以告訴我機場巴士多久一班嗎？

選項：(A) 可以。單程為 120 元。

(B) 可以。它有停靠幾間主要的飯店。

(C) 可以。它每 20 分鐘有一班。

(D) 可以。直走然後左轉。你不會錯過它的。

提示：how often 用以詢問「多常，多久」。

- -

25. I still can't believe my boss fired me!

(A) Wow, she must like you very much!

(B) Gee, I'm sorry to hear that.

(C) Really? Is your boss interesting?

(D) Congratulations. I'm happy for you.

問題：我還是不敢相信我老闆開除了我！

選項：(A) 哇，她一定很喜歡你！

　　　(B) 哎呀，我很抱歉聽到這個消息。

　　　(C) 真的嗎？你的老闆有趣嗎？

　　　(D) 恭喜恭喜。我替你感到高興。

提示：fire 在此當動詞，作「開除，解僱」解。

---

26. How do I get to Gate 18 from here?

(A) Just take the elevator over there to the 2nd floor.

(B) Gate 18 is at Terminal 1, not Terminal 2.

(C) Yes. You'll be boarding at Gate 18.

(D) Your boarding time is 8:30 p.m.

問題：請問要如何從這裡到十八號登機門？

選項：(A) 只要搭那邊的電梯到二樓就可以了。

　　　(B) 十八號登機門在第一航廈，不是第二航廈。

　　　(C) 沒錯。你將在十八號登機門登機。

　　　(D) 你的登機時間為晚上八點半。

---

27. Good morning. Welcome aboard.

(A) Here is your boarding pass.

(B) Yes. I'd like to have some tea, please.

(C) Could you tell me when we'll be boarding?

(D) Hi. Could you show me where seat 34C is?

問題：早安。歡迎登機。

選項：(A) 這是您的登機證。

　　　(B) 是的。我要一些茶，麻煩你了。

　　　(C) 你可以告訴我我們何時登機嗎？

　　　(D) 嗨。你能告訴我座位 34C 在哪裡嗎？

---

28. I have two free tickets for a new action movie. Are you interested?

(A) Yes, it's a great movie.

(B) Cool! Let's go see it.

(C) Sorry, I don't watch romantic movies.

(D) Sure! Science fiction is my favorite.

問題：我有兩張一部新動作片的免費票。你有興趣嗎？

選項：(A) 是的，它是一部很棒的電影。

　　　(B) 好耶！我們一起去看吧。

　　　(C) 抱歉，我不看愛情片。

　　　(D) 當然！科幻小說是我的最愛。

---

29. Do you have a reservation?

(A) Yes. I'll have one beef sandwich and a milk.

(B) Yes. I'd like a single room, please.

(C) Yes. I called six days ago to reserve a room for tonight.

(D) Yes. I'd like to have this skirt washed and ironed.

問題：請問您有預約嗎？

選項：(A) 有。我要一份牛肉三明治與一杯牛奶。

(B) 有。請給我一間單人房。

(C) 有。我六天前打電話預訂今晚的房間。

(D) 有。我想要清洗與熨燙這件裙子。

- -

30. What is your boss like?

(A) He is leaving for Germany tomorrow.

(B) He likes his first company best.

(C) He is not easy to get along with.

(D) He's never talked about it.

問題：你的老闆是個怎樣的人？

選項：(A) 他明天要出發去德國。

(B) 他最喜歡他的第一間公司。

(C) 他不容易相處。

(D) 他從未談論過那件事。

提示：get along with 表「相處」。

31. W: Victoria Hotel.

   M: Hello, my name is Paul Jackson. I've made a room reservation for the sixth this month.

   W: Let me check. That's correct, Mr. Jackson.

   M: I'd like to cancel my reservation for the sixth and change it to the ninth. Would that be possible?

   W: One moment, please. No problem, Mr. Jackson. We'll see you on the ninth.

   Q: What is the man doing?

   (A) Booking a seat on a flight.

   (B) Canceling all of his reservations.

   (C) Leaving a message to a hotel guest.

   (D) Changing the date of his reservation.

   女：Victoria 飯店您好。

   男：哈囉。我是 Paul Jackson。我預訂了這個月六號的房間。

   女：讓我確認一下，沒錯的，Jackson 先生。

   男：我想要取消六號的訂房，改到九號。有可能嗎？

   女：請稍候，沒問題，Jackson 先生。那我們就這個月九號見了。

問題：這個男子在做什麼？

選項：(A) 預訂機位。

(B) 取消他所有的訂房。

(C) 留言給一位房客。

(D) 更改訂房日期。

---

32. M: Ms. Jones! There's a fire in the laboratory!

W: Oh, no. What happened?

M: One student accidentally mixed the wrong chemicals and it exploded.

W: Did you or anyone call the fire department?

Q: Where might this conversation take place?

(A) In a fire department.

(B) In a grocery store.

(C) In a museum.

(D) In a school.

男：Jones 老師！實驗室起火了！

女：哦，不。怎麼回事？

男：有個學生不小心混合了錯的化學藥劑而引發爆炸。

女：你或任何人打電話給消防隊了嗎？

問題：這則對話有可能出現在哪裡？

選項：(A) 消防隊。　　　(B) 雜貨店。

(C) 博物館。　　　(D) 學校。

33. M: Excuse me. Where should I put my bag? It's too big to go under the seat.

W: Have you tried your overhead compartment?

M: Yes, I have. It was full.

W: Let me see. There's still some space in this compartment. Why don't you put your bag in here?

Q: What does the man want to do?

(A) He wants to close the overhead compartment.

(B) He wants a place to put his bag.

(C) He wants his bag to go under his seat.

(D) He wants to empty his bag.

男：不好意思。我應該把我的袋子放哪裡？它太大了，放不進座位底下。

女：你有試過頭上的行李隔層嗎？

男：有，可是它滿了。

女：讓我看看。這個隔層還有一些空間。你何不把袋子放這呢？

問題：這個男子想做什麼？

選項：(A) 他想把行李隔層關上。

(B) 他想要一個地方放袋子。

(C) 他想將袋子放到座位下。

(D) 他想清空他的袋子。

提示：overhead compartment 意指「(機艙內位於座位上) 放行李的隔層」，empty 一字可當形容詞亦可作動詞，當動詞表「把……清空」之意。

---

34. W: I'd like to airmail some printed matter to Europe and Asia.

M: Sure. What kind is it?

W: They are mail order catalogs.

M: OK. Let me check the rate for printed matter.

Q: What does the woman want to mail?

(A) Letters.   (B) Catalogs.

(C) Magazines.   (D) Books.

女：我想要航空郵寄印刷品到歐洲和亞洲。

男：好的。是何種東西？

女：是郵購目錄。

男：沒問題。讓我查一下印刷品的郵資。

問題：這個女子要郵寄什麼？

選項：(A) 信件。   (B) 目錄。

　　　(C) 雜誌。   (D) 書。

35. M: Here you go. 3,000 pounds all in 50-pound notes.

W: Thanks. Could I have an envelope to put it in?

M: No problem. Here you are.

W: Thank you.

Q: How did the woman want her money?

(A) In 50-pound bills.

(B) In 20-pound bills.

(C) In 10-pound bills.

(D) In 5-pound bills.

男：這是你的三千英鎊，全部是面額五十英鎊的鈔票。

女：謝謝。可以給我個信封裝錢嗎？

男：沒問題。拿去吧。

女：謝謝你。

問題：這個女子要什麼面額的鈔票？

選項：(A) 五十英鎊的鈔票。

　　　(B) 二十英鎊的鈔票。

　　　(C) 十英鎊的鈔票。

　　　(D) 五英鎊的鈔票。

提示：bill 與 note 在此皆作「紙幣，鈔票」解。bill 為美式用法，note 則為英式用法。

36. M: What's the problem?

W: I think my baby has a fever.

M: When did it start?

W: About two hours ago. She just kept crying.

M: OK. Let me take a look at her.

Q: Which is true?

(A) The woman is a doctor.

(B) The baby got hurt.

(C) The man will examine the baby.

(D) They are in a fire station.

男：怎麼了呢？

女：我想我的寶寶發燒了。

男：什麼時候開始的？

女：大概兩小時前。她一直在哭。

男：好的。讓我看看她吧。

問題：何者屬實？

選項：(A) 這位女子是醫生。

(B) 這個寶寶受傷了。

(C) 這個男子會檢查寶寶。

(D) 他們在消防站裡。

⸺⸺⸺⸺⸺⸺⸺⸺⸺⸺⸺⸺⸺⸺⸺⸺⸺⸺

37. M: Excuse me. I think I lost your book. It's *The Handbook of Joy*.

W: May I have your name, please?

M: Ian Thomas.

W: Well, Mr. Thomas. You'll have to buy a copy of the same book and give it to the library.

Q: What will the man have to do?

(A) Ask the woman to pay him money.

(B) Ask the library to buy a book for him.

(C) Return his library card to the library.

(D) Buy a copy of *The Handbook of Joy*.

男：不好意思。我想我弄丟了你們的書。是《喜悅指南》這一本。

女：請給我你的名字好嗎？

男：Ian Thomas。

女：嗯，Thomas 先生，你必須要買一本同樣的書歸還給圖書館。

問題：這個男子將必須做什麼？

選項：(A) 要求女子付他錢。

(B) 要求圖書館幫他買一本書。

(C) 將他的借書證還給圖書館。

(D) 買一本《喜悅指南》。

---

38. M: I really enjoyed the movie.

W: I'm glad to hear that. I think it's a good story.

M: Yes. I can't imagine if I had to go through

what the character had to. I probably
wouldn't be able to survive.

W: Me neither. Some people are just stronger
than others.

Q: What did the man and woman like about
the movie?

(A) The beginning.　　(B) The story.

(C) The music.　　(D) The ending.

男：我真的很喜歡這部電影。

女：我很開心聽到你這麼說。我覺得它的故事很棒。

男：沒錯。我無法想像如何渡過主角所經歷的難關。
我大概沒有辦法存活下來。

女：我也是。有一些人就是比別人要堅強多了。

問題：這個男子與女子喜歡這部電影的什麼？

選項：(A) 開頭。　　(B) 故事。

　　　(C) 音樂。　　(D) 結局。

- -

39. W: What's wrong?

M: I feel dizzy.

W: Why don't you try something sweet? It
works for me every time.

M: Really? I have a chocolate bar. I'll give it a
try.

Q: What did the woman suggest to the man?

(A) Trying some sweets.

(B) Giving her some chocolate.

(C) Going to a doctor.

(D) Stopping eating chocolate.

女：怎麼了？

男：我覺得頭暈。

女：你何不吃些甜的東西？我每次吃都有效。

男：真的嗎？我有一條巧克力棒。我會試試看的。

問題：這個女子建議男子什麼？

選項：(A) 吃一些甜食。

　　　(B) 給她一些巧克力。

　　　(C) 去看醫生。

　　　(D) 停止吃巧克力。

---

40. W: What is it, John? You haven't been like yourself these last couple of days.

M: Oh, don't remind me. Betty and I broke up. She left me for another man.

W: I'm sorry to hear that. I can well understand your feelings. I felt terrible when Mark left me. But trust me, you'll get over it.

M: I hope so. But thanks for the encouragement.

Q: How did the woman encourage the man?

(A) She reminded him to see a doctor.

(B) She told him the same thing had happened to her.

(C) She would introduce her friend to him.

(D) She would take a week's vacation with him.

女：怎麼啦，John？你過去這幾天不太像你哦。

男：噢，別說了。Betty 跟我分手了。她為了別的男子離開了我。

女：我很抱歉聽到這件事。我很能了解你的感受。當 Mark 離開我時我也覺得糟透了。不過相信我，你會好起來的。

男：希望如此。但還是謝謝你的鼓勵。

問題：這個女子如何鼓勵男子？

選項：(A) 她提醒他要去看醫生。

　　　(B) 她告訴他同樣的事也曾發生在她身上。

　　　(C) 她會介紹她的朋友給他認識。

　　　(D) 她會跟他一起去渡一星期的假。

提示：get over 在此作「恢復過來，(在一件不開心的事結束後)重新快樂起來」。

41. W: I'm paying for this meal.

　　M: No. It should be my treat.

　　W: Please. I was the one who invited you for dinner.

M: OK. If you insist.

Q. What were they arguing about?

(A) How to treat each other.

(B) Where to have dinner.

(C) Who was to pay the bill.

(D) Who was to be invited for dinner.

女：我來付這頓飯的錢。

男：不，應該是我請你。

女：拜託。是我邀你吃晚餐的耶。

男：好吧。如果你堅持的話。

問題：他們在爭論什麼？

選項：(A) 如何對待對方。

　　　(B) 去哪裡吃晚餐。

　　　(C) 誰來付帳單。

　　　(D) 要邀請誰吃晚餐。

- -

42. M: Did you watch the swimming contest yesterday?

W: No. I went out with my parents to visit my grandparents. How did it go?

M: It was very exciting. Thanks to our new coach, our swimming club took first place. Too bad you didn't see it.

W: Yeah! What a pity!

Q: What had happened yesterday?

(A) The girl's parents were sick.

(B) The boy's swimming club won first prize.

(C) The swimming club changed their coach.

(D) The girl went to see the swimming contest.

男：你有看昨天的游泳比賽嗎？

女：沒有。我跟我爸媽出門去拜訪我祖父母了。比賽
　　如何？

男：很刺激。多虧我們的新教練，我們游泳社得到第
　　一名。真遺憾你沒有看到。

女：是啊！真的很可惜！

問題：昨天發生了什麼事？

選項：(A) 這個女孩的父母生病了。

　　　(B) 這個男孩的游泳社得到比賽第一名。

　　　(C) 這個游泳社換掉了他們的教練。

　　　(D) 這個女孩去看了游泳比賽。

提示：thanks to 表「多虧，幸好」；too bad 為口語
　　　用法，表示「遺憾，可惜」；what a pity 亦作
　　　「真可惜」解。

- -

43. W: My sister and I are thinking of going on a
　　　trip to South Africa. Are you interested?

　　M: South Africa? What will you do there?

　　W: We want to go to their national park to see

the wild animals.

M: Well, I'm not interested in that sort of thing. But thanks for asking anyway.

Q: Which is true?

(A) The man will go to South Africa with the woman.

(B) The man is interested in visiting South Africa.

(C) The woman is interested in wild animals.

(D) The woman has been to South Africa.

女：我和我姊姊想要去南非旅遊。你有興趣嗎？

男：南非？你們會在那裡做什麼？

女：我們想去它的國家公園看那些野生動物。

男：嗯，我對那個沒有興趣。不過還是謝謝你問我。

問題：何者屬實？

選項：(A) 這個男子會和女子一起去南非。

　　　(B) 這個男子有興趣去南非。

　　　(C) 這個女子對野生動物有興趣。

　　　(D) 這個女子已經去過南非。

44. M: Hello, I bought a TV from your store and I don't think it's working too well.

W: Could you tell me what the problem is?

M: The sound is interrupted for certain

stations.

W: I see. I'll contact the manufacturer and will get back to you as soon as I have some information.

Q: Who did the man call?

(A) The store where he bought the TV.

(B) The cable TV operator.

(C) The TV manufacturer.

(D) The TV station.

男：哈囉，我在你們店裡買了一臺電視，我覺得它有點故障。

女：你能跟我說一下問題是什麼嗎？

男：有幾個電視臺的聲音有干擾。

女：我了解了。我連絡廠商得到資訊後會盡快與你連絡。

問題：這個男子打電話給誰？

選項：(A) 他購買電視的商家。

(B) 電視天線操作員。

(C) 製造電視的廠商。

(D) 電視臺。

---

45. M: Good morning. How can I help you?

W: Yes. I'd like to buy 500 dollars in cash, and 500 dollars in traveler's checks.

M: Sure. Please fill out this form. Do you have your ID with you?

W: Yes. Here you are.

Q: How much does the woman want to buy?

(A) 500 dollars.   (B) 2,000 dollars.

(C) 1,500 dollars.   (D) 1,000 dollars.

男：早安。我能為您服務嗎？

女：是的。我想要買美金 500 元現金，還有美金 500 元旅行支票。

男：沒問題。請填寫這張表格。您有帶著您的身分證嗎？

女：有的。在這裡。

問題：這個女子總共買了多少美金？

選項：(A) 500 元美金。

      (B) 2,000 元美金。

      (C) 1,500 元美金。

      (D) 1,000 元美金。

此部分有 15 題，每題都有一張與該題目相對應的圖畫。請聽錄音機播出題目以及 A、B、C、D 四個英語敘述之後，選出與所看到的圖畫最相符的答案。每題只播出一遍。

1 ___

2 ___

3 ___

4 _____

5 _____

6 _____

Bulletin Board

Yangming College Admission Test Reporting—in times

Time	Groups
8:30 ~ 9:00	Group A1, Group A2
9:30 ~ 10:00	Group B1, Group B2
13:00 ~ 13:30	Group C1, Group C2
14:00 ~ 14:30	Group D1, Group D2

7 _____

8 ___

9 ___

10 ___

11 ___

12 _____

Sherwood Taipei	
Billing Name: Albert Lee	
Arrival Date: 2005/11/19	
Departure Date: 2005/11/21	
Room No.: 601 Persons: 2	
11/19 Room Charge	4,000
11/19 Service Charge	400
11/20 Room Charge	4,000
11/20 Service Charge	400
Total	8,800

13 _____

14 _____

15 _____

此部分有 15 題，每題請聽錄音機播出一個英語句子之後，從 A、B、C、D 四個回答或回應中，選出一個最適合者作答。每題只播出一遍。

_____ 16 (A) In two weeks.

(B) It is not mine.

(C) The fine is one NT dollar a day.

(D) You can borrow two books at a time.

_____ 17 (A) You have to work out to keep fit.

(B) My dad will kill me if he finds out.

(C) It won't kill you to help me a little.

(D) Maybe you should take a vacation.

_____ 18 (A) No. I don't have any questions about you.

(B) Sorry. I don't know the answer to your question.

(C) Sure. You ask whatever you want to know about.

(D) Yes. I'd like to know about your scholarship program.

19 (A) I just joined the guitar club.

(B) I'm late for basketball practice.

(C) I can't talk to you right now.

(D) I got here a few minutes ago.

20 (A) I live in Taipei.

(B) I enjoy my life.

(C) I'm an engineer.

(D) I'm on vacation.

21 (A) Really? You can help me.

(B) Why? Is there something wrong?

(C) Sure. You deserve a better man.

(D) That's great. I'm glad you like it.

22 (A) My father will be fifty years old next week.

(B) My father always keeps me company.

(C) Well, almost three years.

(D) Sure, I enjoy my work.

23 (A) Sounds great. I love that Italian restaurant.
(B) Good idea. I need a break from my work.
(C) No way. I haven't been to Italy before.
(D) Thanks for your offer. I can do it myself.

24 (A) I don't mind sleeping alone.
(B) No, I'll phone you again.
(C) That's very kind of you.
(D) That'll be fine. I'll take it.

25 (A) That's great. I am Ted Smith.
(B) That's alright. Thank you.
(C) I'll check other airlines, thanks.
(D) I'll take a double room, then.

26 (A) Sure. When would you like to go?
(B) OK. How many people do you have?
(C) I'm not sure. Could you bring me the menu again?
(D) I'm sorry. Your reservation has

been canceled.

27 (A) Yes. I have one bag.
(B) Yes. I can carry it myself.
(C) No. I don't need them.
(D) No. I'm leaving now.

28 (A) Flight 206 is about to board.
(B) The boarding time is 1:00 p.m.
(C) The flight is to London.
(D) Gate 25. Have a nice trip.

29 (A) Sure. What would you like to eat?
(B) No problem. Which one do you prefer?
(C) Sure. I'll get some coffee for you.
(D) Hold on. I'll bring you some medicine.

30 (A) Sure. I think you can find it by yourself.
(B) Sure. Just keep walking, and it's on your left.
(C) Sorry. You are sitting on my seat.
(D) Sorry. I can't tell you anything about it.

此部分有 15 題，每題請聽錄音機播出一段對話及一個相關的問題，然後從 A、B、C、D 四個選項中挑出一個最適合的答案。每題只播出一遍。

_____ 31 (A) Picking up a book at the library.
(B) Holding a meeting.
(C) Leaving a message to Ms. Jones.
(D) Checking in at a hotel.

_____ 32 (A) One book.　　(B) Five books.
(C) Six books.　　(D) Seven books.

_____ 33 (A) Their great customer service.
(B) Their interior decoration.
(C) The simple design of their furniture.
(D) The quality and prices of their goods.

_____ 34 (A) Its price.　　(B) Its style.
(C) Its color.　　(D) Its size.

_____ 35 (A) She didn't have any neighbors.
(B) She had to move to a new

apartment.

(C) Her neighbor is too noisy at night.

(D) Her furniture is too heavy for her to move.

___ 36 (A) Going to a pub at night.

(B) Joining the music club.

(C) Buying a live concert ticket.

(D) Starting a music club at school.

___ 37 (A) Apply for a college.

(B) Get a job.

(C) Find a new secretary.

(D) Leave a message.

___ 38 (A) The woman wanted to quit.

(B) The woman wanted a raise.

(C) Mr. Lee was the woman's boss.

(D) Mr. Lee was unhappy about the news.

___ 39 (A) She bought an old house in England.

(B) She wants to study English in England.

(C) She has friends living in England.

(D) She is interested in historic buildings.

40 (A) 6 a.m. flight. (B) 9 a.m. flight.

(C) 6 p.m. flight. (D) 2 p.m. flight.

41 (A) US$50. (B) US$90.

(C) US$100. (D) US$110.

42 (A) An aisle seat at the front.

(B) A window seat at the front.

(C) An aisle seat at the back.

(D) A window seat at the back.

43 (A) His watch. (B) His passport.

(C) His ticket. (D) His backpack.

44 (A) Stop singing. (B) Stop smoking.

(C) Stop reading. (D) Stop talking.

45 (A) Lay his bag in the aisle.

(B) Put down his tray table.

(C) Put his bag under the seat in front of him.

(D) Go back to his seat and fasten his seat belt.

1. What is the girl doing?

  (A) Giving a library book back.

  (B) Mailing a book to the library.

  (C) Donating a book to the library.

  (D) Borrowing a library book.

  問題：這個女孩正在做什麼？

  選項：(A) 還圖書館的書。

  　　　(B) 寄書給圖書館。

  　　　(C) 捐書給圖書館。

  　　　(D) 借圖書館的書。

- -

2. How often does the library have someone tell stories?

  (A) Once a week.　　　(B) Twice a week.

  (C) Three times a week.　(D) Four times a week.

  問題：這間圖書館多久有人說故事？

  選項：(A) 一週一次。　　(B) 一週兩次。

  　　　(C) 一週三次。　　(D) 一週四次。

  提示：說故事時間是週二和週五。

- -

3. What does the woman think about the food?

(A) So-so. (B) Delicious.

(C) Terrible. (D) Strange.

問題：這個女子覺得食物如何？

選項：(A) 馬馬虎虎。 (B) 很美味。

　　　(C) 糟透了。 (D) 很奇怪。

---

4. Which is true?

(A) The woman is angry about what has happened.

(B) The man is sorry about what has happened.

(C) The woman's car hit the man's at the back.

(D) The man's car isn't damaged at all.

問題：何者屬實？

選項：(A) 女子對於剛發生的事感到生氣。

　　　(B) 男子對於剛發生的事感到抱歉。

　　　(C) 女子的車從後方撞上男子的車。

　　　(D) 男子的車沒有絲毫的毀損。

---

5. What is happening in the picture?

(A) The baby drew pictures on the wall.

(B) The man and the woman are quarrelling.

(C) The woman is picking the baby up.

(D) The baby is learning how to walk.

問題：圖中發生什麼事？

選項：(A) 小寶寶在牆上塗鴉。

(B) 男子和女子正在吵架。

(C) 女子正將小寶寶抱起。

(D) 小寶寶正在學走路。

6. When should people of Group C1 report?

(A) 8:30 a.m. to 9:00 a.m.

(B) 9:30 a.m. to 10:00 a.m.

(C) 1:00 p.m. to 1:30 p.m.

(D) 2:00 p.m. to 2:30 p.m.

問題：C1 組的人應該何時報到？

選項：(A) 上午八點半到九點。

(B) 上午九點半到十點。

(C) 下午一點到一點半。

(D) 下午兩點到兩點半。

7. Which might be the question that the professors asked?

(A) Could you tell us more about yourself?

(B) Why do you want to major in English?

(C) Did your family come here with you?

(D) How do you like our school?

問題：哪個可能是教授們問的問題？

選項：(A) 可以告訴我們多一點關於你的事嗎？

(B) 你為什麼想要主修英文？

(C) 你的家人有和你一起來嗎？

(D) 你覺得我們學校如何呢？

提示：男生在談的是家人，所以問題應該和他本身有關。

---

8. What was the professor's question?

(A) Who is your favorite teacher?

(B) Did you join any school clubs?

(C) Could you tell us about your family?

(D) Why do you want to attend our school?

問題：教授的問題是什麼？

選項：(A) 誰是你最喜歡的老師？

(B) 你有參加過任何學校社團嗎？

(C) 可以跟我們談談你的家人嗎？

(D) 你為什麼想要進入我們學校？

---

9. What does the man do?

(A) He is a salesman.　　(B) He is a mailman.

(C) He is a waiter.　　(D) He is a reporter.

問題：這個男子從事什麼行業？

選項：(A) 他是銷售員。　　(B) 他是郵差。

(C) 他是服務生。　　(D) 他是記者。

10. What organization are the men working for?

    (A) A hospital emergency room.

    (B) A fire department.

    (C) A cleaning company.

    (D) A police department.

    問題：這些男子替什麼機關工作？

    選項：(A) 醫院急診室。　(B) 消防局。

    　　　(C) 清潔公司。　　(D) 警察局。

---

11. What does the girl want to know?

    (A) The room rates.

    (B) The room service.

    (C) The laundry service.

    (D) The transportation services.

    問題：這個女生想要知道什麼？

    選項：(A) 房間價格。　　(B) 客房服務。

    　　　(C) 洗衣服務。　　(D) 交通服務。

    提示：deluxe suite 為「豪華套房」；standard suite
    　　　為「標準套房」；double 在此表「雙人房」。

---

12. How long did the guests stay in this hotel?

    (A) One night.　　　　(B) Two nights.

    (C) Four nights.　　　(D) Six nights.

    問題：房客在這間飯店住了多久？

選項：(A) 一個晚上。　　(B) 兩個晚上。
　　　(C) 四個晚上。　　(D) 六個晚上。

提示：住了 11 月 19 日和 11 月 20 日兩個晚上。

---

13. What would the man probably say to the woman?

(A) I'd like to book a table for two.

(B) I'd like to sit in the smoking area.

(C) I'd like a table by the window, if possible.

(D) I'd like a glass of red wine, please.

問題：這個男子可能對女子說什麼？

選項：(A) 我想要訂兩個人的位子。

　　　(B) 我想要坐在吸煙區。

　　　(C) 可能的話，我想要靠窗的位子。

　　　(D) 麻煩請給我一杯紅酒。

---

14. When can the people board the plane?

(A) After 30 minutes.　　(B) After 20 minutes.

(C) After 15 minutes.　　(D) After 10 minutes.

問題：這些人何時可以登機？

選項：(A) 30 分鐘後。　　(B) 20 分鐘後。

　　　(C) 15 分鐘後。　　(D) 10 分鐘後。

提示：時鐘顯示時間為 6 點 20 分，離登機時間尚有
　　　10 分鐘。

15. What is the woman saying to the flight attendant?

(A) When will the first meal be served?

(B) What would you like for breakfast?

(C) May I have a glass of water?

(D) May I see the catalog?

問題：這個女子在對空服人員說什麼？

選項：(A) 第一餐何時供應？

(B) 您的早餐想要點什麼？

(C) 可以給我一杯水嗎？

(D) 我可以看一下目錄嗎？

第二部分 腳本與解析 Track #14

16. When should this book be returned?

(A) In two weeks.

(B) It is not mine.

(C) The fine is one NT dollar a day.

(D) You can borrow two books at a time.

問題：這本書何時該歸還？

選項：(A) 兩個星期內。

(B) 那不是我的。

(C) 罰款一天新臺幣一元。

(D) 你一次可以借兩本書。

提示：fine 在此作名詞，為「罰緩，罰款」之意。

---

17. I'm really stressed out. My work is killing me.

(A) You have to work out to keep fit.

(B) My dad will kill me if he finds out.

(C) It won't kill you to help me a little.

(D) Maybe you should take a vacation.

問題：我真的累壞了。我的工作真是要我的命。

選項：(A) 你必須健身以維持身體健康。

(B) 我爸如果發現了會殺了我。

(C) 幫我一點忙不會害了你。

(D) 或許你該去渡個假。

---

18. Do you have any questions?

(A) No. I want to know the answer.

(B) Sorry. I don't know the answer to your question.

(C) Sure. You ask whatever you want to know about.

(D) Yes. I'd like to know about your scholarship program.

問題：你有任何問題嗎？

選項：(A) 不。我想知道答案。

　　　(B) 抱歉。我不知道你問題的答案。

　　　(C) 當然。你可以問任何想知道的事情。

　　　(D) 是的。我想知道你們的獎學金計畫。

---

19. Hey, what's the hurry?

(A) I just joined the guitar club.

(B) I'm late for basketball practice.

(C) I can't talk to you right now.

(D) I got here a few minutes ago.

問題：嘿，什麼事這麼急？

選項：(A) 我剛加入了吉他社。

　　　(B) 我籃球練習遲到了。

　　　(C) 我現在不能跟你說話。

　　　(D) 我幾分鐘前才到這裡。

---

20. What do you do for a living?

(A) I live in Taipei.　　　(B) I enjoy my life.

(C) I'm an engineer.　　　(D) I'm on vacation.

問題：你從事什麼行業？

選項：(A) 我住在臺北。

　　　(B) 我喜歡我的生活。

　　　(C) 我是工程師。

　　　(D) 我正在渡假。

提示：“What do you do for a living?” = “What do you do as a job?” = “What are you?”，表示「你從事什麼行業？」或是「你的職業是什麼？」。

---

21. I'm thinking of changing my job.

(A) Really? You can help me.

(B) Why? Is there something wrong?

(C) Sure. You deserve a better man.

(D) That's great. I'm glad you like it.

問題：我在考慮更換我的工作。

選項：(A) 真的嗎？你可以幫我。

　　　(B) 為什麼？怎麼了嗎？

　　　(C) 當然。你值得更好的男人。

　　　(D) 那太好了。我很高興你喜歡它。

---

22. How long have you been working in your father's company?

(A) My father will be fifty years old next week.

(B) My father always keeps me company.

(C) Well, almost three years.

(D) Sure, I enjoy my work.

問題：你在你爸爸的公司工作多久了？

選項：(A) 我爸爸下星期就要滿五十歲了。

(B) 我爸爸總是陪著我。

(C) 嗯，快三年了。

(D) 當然，我喜歡我的工作。

---

23. Let's visit southern Italy this summer vacation.

(A) Sounds great. I love that Italian restaurant.

(B) Good idea. I need a break from my work.

(C) No way. I haven't been to Italy before.

(D) Thanks for your offer. I can do it myself.

問題：我們這個暑假去南義大利玩吧。

選項：(A) 聽起來很棒。我愛死那家義大利餐廳了。

　　　(B) 好主意。我需要從工作中喘口氣。

　　　(C) 不行。我從來沒有去過義大利。

　　　(D) 謝謝你的提議。我可以自己來。

提示：break 作名詞用，表示「休息」的意思。

---

24. We only have one single room left. Do you mind facing the street?

(A) I don't mind sleeping alone.

(B) No, I'll phone you again.

(C) That's very kind of you.

(D) That'll be fine. I'll take it.

問題：我們只剩一間單人房。你介意面向街道嗎？

選項：(A) 我不介意一個人睡。

(B) 不會，我會再打電話給你。

(C) 你真好心。

(D) 沒關係。我要了。

---

25. I'm sorry. Our hotel is fully booked.

(A) That's great. I am Ted Smith.

(B) That's alright. Thank you.

(C) I'll check other airlines, thanks.

(D) I'll take a double room, then.

問題：抱歉。我們飯店已經客滿了。

選項：(A) 太棒了。我叫 Ted Smith。

(B) 沒關係。謝謝你。

(C) 我會查別家航空公司，謝謝。

(D) 那麼我要一間雙人房。

---

26. Hello, I'd like to book five seats on the morning flight to Tokyo, please.

(A) Sure. When would you like to go?

(B) OK. How many people do you have?

(C) I'm not sure. Could you bring me the menu again?

(D) I'm sorry. Your reservation has been canceled.

問題：你好，麻煩你，我想要預訂五個飛東京的早班

機機位。

選項：(A) 好的。你想要什麼時候出發？

(B) 好的。你們有多少人？

(C) 我不確定。你可以再給我菜單嗎？

(D) 很抱歉，你的預約已被取消。

---

27. Do you have any bags to check in?

(A) Yes. I have one bag.

(B) Yes. I can carry it myself.

(C) No. I don't need them.

(D) No. I'm leaving now.

問題：你有任何要託運的包包嗎？

選項：(A) 是的。我有一個包包。

(B) 是的。我可以自己提。

(C) 沒有。我不需要它們。

(D) 沒有。我現在要離開了。

提示：check in 為「託運」的意思，通常搭飛機時，
過大、過重的行李均需要拖運，不可帶進機艙。

---

28. Which gate will the flight be boarding?

(A) Flight 206 is about to board.

(B) The boarding time is 1:00 p.m.

(C) The flight is to London.

(D) Gate 25. Have a nice trip.

問題：這班飛機要在幾號登機門登機？

選項：(A) 206 班機即將開始登機。

(B) 登機時間是下午一點。

(C) 這班飛機是去倫敦的。

(D) 25 號機門。祝你旅途愉快。

---

29. Excuse me. I got a stomach ache. Do you have anything I could take?

(A) Sure. What would you like to eat?

(B) No problem. Which one do you prefer?

(C) Sure. I'll get some coffee for you.

(D) Hold on. I'll bring you some medicine.

問題：不好意思。我胃在痛。你有任何我能服用的藥物嗎？

選項：(A) 當然。你想要吃什麼？

(B) 沒問題。你喜歡哪一個？

(C) 當然。我幫你倒一些咖啡。

(D) 等一下。我拿一些藥給你。

---

30. Could you tell me where seat 27B is?

(A) Sure. I think you can find it by yourself.

(B) Sure. Just keep walking, and it's on your left.

(C) Sorry. You are sitting on my seat.

(D) Sorry. I can't tell you anything about it.

問題：你能告訴我座位 27B 在哪嗎？

選項：(A) 當然。我想你可以靠自己找到它。

(B) 當然。繼續往前走，它在你的左手邊。

(C) 抱歉。你坐到我的位子了。

(D) 抱歉。我無法告訴你任何關於它的事情。

提示：on one's right/left 表示「在某人的右或左手邊」。

第三部分　**腳本與解析**

Track #15

31. W: Hi, I'd like to get the book you held for me two days ago.

M: May I have your name?

W: Amy Jones.

M: Let me see. Yes. Here you go.

Q: What was the woman doing?

(A) Picking up a book at the library.

(B) Holding a meeting.

(C) Leaving a message to Ms. Jones.

(D) Checking in at a hotel.

女：你好，我想拿你們兩天前幫我保留的書。

男：能給我你的名字嗎？

女：Amy Jones。

男：讓我查查。有的，這是你的書。

問題：這個女子在做什麼？

選項：(A) 在圖書館取書。

(B) 舉辦一個會議。

(C) 留言給 Jones 小姐。

(D) 在飯店辦理登記入宿。

提示：對話裡的 hold 為「保留」之意，也可以 reserve 替代。

---

32. W: Excuse me. Can I check out one more book?

M: I'm sorry. The most you can borrow is six books at a time.

W: I see. I'll put this book back.

Q: How many books did the woman borrow?

(A) One book.   (B) Five books.

(C) Six books.   (D) Seven books.

女：不好意思。我可以再多借一本書嗎？

男：很抱歉。一次最多只能借六本書。

女：我知道了。我會將這本書放回去。

問題：這個女子借了幾本書？

選項：(A) 一本書。   (B) 五本書。

(C) 六本書。   (D) 七本書。

---

33. W: Thanks for recommending that furniture

store to me.

M: I'm glad you liked it. Did you find anything you need?

W: Yes, I did. The quality of the furniture is good, and the price is very reasonable as well.

Q: What does the woman like about the store?

(A) Their great customer service.

(B) Their interior decoration.

(C) The simple design of their furniture.

(D) The quality and prices of their goods.

女：謝謝你推薦我那家傢俱店。

男：我很高興妳喜歡它。妳有找到任何需要的東西嗎？

女：有，我有。它們傢俱的品質很好，價錢也很合理。

問題：這個女子喜歡這家店的什麼？

選項：(A) 它們良好的顧客服務。

　　　(B) 它們的內部裝潢。

　　　(C) 它們傢俱的簡單設計。

　　　(D) 它們產品的品質和價錢。

---

34. M: I think this T-shirt looks quite nice on you.

W: Really? Don't you think it's a bit tight?

M: Well, if you don't feel comfortable in it, why

don't you try a larger one?

Q: What does the woman dislike about the T-shirt?

(A) Its price.   (B) Its style.

(C) Its color.   (D) Its size.

男：我覺得這件 T 恤你穿起來很好看。

女：真的嗎？你不覺得有點太緊了嗎？

男：嗯，如果你覺得穿起來不舒服，何不試試大一點的？

問題：這個女子不喜歡這件 T 恤的什麼？

選項：(A) 它的價錢。   (B) 它的款式。

       (C) 它的顏色。   (D) 它的尺寸。

---

35. M: What's bothering you, Sandra?

W: It's the new neighbor right above my apartment. He keeps moving his furniture around at night. The noise is driving me crazy.

M: Maybe you should have a talk with him. I can go with you if you want.

W: That'd be great. Thanks.

Q: What was the woman's problem?

(A) She didn't have any neighbors.

(B) She had to move to a new apartment.

(C) Her neighbor is too noisy at night.

(D) Her furniture is too heavy for her to move.

男：Sandra，有什麼事讓你困擾嗎？

女：是住在我公寓樓上的新鄰居。他不斷在晚上將傢俱移來移去。那噪音快把我弄瘋了。

男：或許你該和他談一談。如果你想要，我可以陪你一起去。

女：那真是太好了。謝謝。

問題：這個女子的問題是什麼？

選項：(A) 她沒有任何鄰居。

(B) 她必須搬去新的公寓。

(C) 她的鄰居晚上太吵了。

(D) 她的傢俱對她來說太重，以至於她搬不動。

36. W: I was wondering if your music club collects any fees.

M: Yes. We collect seven dollars each semester.

W: How often do you meet?

M: Once a week.

Q: What was the woman interested in?

(A) Going to a pub at night.

(B) Joining the music club.

(C) Buying a live concert ticket.

(D) Starting a music club at school.

女：我想知道音樂社是否有收任何費用？

男：有的。我們每學期收七美元。

女：你們多久聚會一次？

男：一星期一次。

問題：這個女子對什麼感興趣？

選項：(A) 在晚上去酒吧。

(B) 參加音樂社。

(C) 買現場音樂會門票。

(D) 在學校成立音樂社。

提示：女子詢問了關於音樂社的事情，由此可推知她對這個社團有興趣，想要進一步得知相關訊息，故本題應選(B)。

---

37. M: Look, here's a perfect job for you.

W: What is it?

M: It says secretary wanted: female with college degree. Experience is not required. If interested, call 555-9843.

W: Sounds good. I'll give them a call right away.

Q: What is the woman trying to do?

(A) Apply for a college.

(B) Get a job.

(C) Find a new secretary.

(D) Leave a message.

男：看，這裡有一個適合你的工作。

女：是什麼？

男：它寫徵求秘書：有大學學歷的女性，經驗不拘。
若有興趣，請洽 555-9843。

女：聽起來不錯。我馬上打電話過去。

問題：這個女子試著做什麼？

選項：(A) 申請大學。　　(B) 得到工作。
　　　(C) 找到新秘書。　(D) 留言。

---

38. M: What do you mean you want to quit? I
won't allow it.

W: But Mr. Lee, I really need to spend more
time with my family.

M: I can't lose you. You're too important to this
company.

W: I'm sorry. But anything you say will not
change my mind.

Q: Which is NOT true?

(A) The woman wanted to quit.

(B) The woman wanted a raise.

(C) Mr. Lee was the woman's boss.

(D) Mr. Lee was unhappy about the news.

男：你說要辭職是什麼意思？我不會允許的。

女：但是 Lee 先生，我真的需要多花點時間陪我的家

　　　　人。

男：我不能失去你。你對這間公司太重要了。

女：我很抱歉。但是任何你說的事情都無法讓我改變
　　主意。

問題：何者不屬實？

選項：(A) 這個女子想要辭職。

　　　(B) 這個女子想要加薪。

　　　(C) Lee 先生是這個女子的老闆。

　　　(D) Lee 先生因此消息感到不高興。

---

39. W: I hope I can visit England someday.

M: Well, I feel the same way.

W: There are many historic buildings in
　　England. I'm always fascinated by them.

M: I couldn't agree more.

Q: Why would the woman want to visit
　　England?

(A) She bought an old house in England.

(B) She wants to study English in England.

(C) She has friends living in England.

(D) She is interested in historic buildings.

女：我希望有一天我可以去英國。

男：嗯，我也這麼希望。

女：英國有許多歷史悠久的建築，我總是對它們深深

著迷。

男：我非常同意你的看法。

問題：這個女子為什麼想要去英國？

選項：(A) 她在英國買了間老房子。

(B) 她想去英國研讀英文。

(C) 她有朋友住在英國。

(D) 她對歷史建築有興趣。

----

40. W: Phoenix Airways. May I help you?

M: Yes, I'd like to book a flight to London on August 1st.

W: OK. We have two flights to London on that day, one at 9 a.m. and the other at 6 p.m. Which would you prefer?

M: The night flight, please.

Q: Which flight will the man take?

(A) 6 a.m. flight.　　　　(B) 9 a.m. flight.

(C) 6 p.m. flight.　　　　(D) 2 p.m. flight.

女：Phoenix 航空。我能為您效勞嗎？

男：是的，我想要預訂八月一日當天前往倫敦的班機。

女：好的。我們那天有兩班飛往倫敦的班機，一班在早上九點，另一班則在晚上六點。請問您想要搭乘哪一班？

男：晚上那班，謝謝。

問題：這個男子會搭哪一班飛機？

選項：(A) 早上六點的班機。

(B) 早上九點的班機。

(C) 晚上六點的班機。

(D) 晚上兩點的班機。

---

41. M: Good afternoon, Ocean View Hotel. May I help you?

W: Yes. I'd like to know how much you charge for a double room.

M: It's US$50 per night. How many rooms do you need?

W: Two. Could you give me a better rate?

M: Sure. I can take 10% off.

W: Great. I'd like to reserve two rooms for this weekend.

Q: How much will the woman pay?

(A) US$50.   (B) US$90.

(C) US$100.   (D) US$110.

男：午安，Ocean View 飯店。我能為您效勞嗎？

女：是的。我想要知道你們雙人房的房價。

男：一晚 50 美元。您需要幾間房呢？

女：兩間。你能給我們較便宜的價格嗎？

男：當然。我可以幫您打九折。

女：太棒了。我想要預訂這個週末的兩間房。

問題：這個女子將付多少錢？

選項：(A) 50 美元。　　(B) 90 美元。
　　　(C) 100 美元。　　(D) 110 美元。

提示：take 10% off 即「打九折」，一間房一晚 50 美
　　　元，兩間房即是 100 美元；再乘上 0.9，可知
　　　這個女子須付 90 美元。

---

42. M: Do you have any seating preference?

W: I'd like to have a window seat, please.

M: Sure. Let me see. Do you mind sitting at the
　　back?

W: Not at all.

Q: Where will the woman be sitting?

(A) An aisle seat at the front.

(B) A window seat at the front.

(C) An aisle seat at the back.

(D) A window seat at the back.

男：你有任何偏好的座位嗎？

女：我想要靠窗的座位，謝謝。

男：好的，讓我看看。你介意坐在後面嗎？

女：一點也不。

問題：這個女子會坐在哪裡？

43. W: May I have your passport, please?

M: Sure...oh, no, I can't find it.

W: Take your time. Maybe you can check your backpack.

M: Let me see. Yes, here it is. There you go.

Q: What was the man looking for?

(A) His watch.　　　　(B) His passport.

(C) His ticket.　　　　(D) His backpack.

女：能給我你的護照嗎？

男：當然……喔，不，我找不到它。

女：慢慢來。或許你可以在你的背包裡找找。

男：讓我看看。有了，在這裡。拿去吧。

問題：這個男子在找什麼？

選項：(A) 他的手錶。　　(B) 他的護照。

(C) 他的機票。　　(D) 他的背包。

44. W: Excuse me, sir. You can't smoke in the cabin.

M: Oh, I'm very sorry. I'll put it out right away.

W: Thank you.

Q: What did the woman ask the man to do?

(A) Stop singing.　　　　(B) Stop smoking.

(C) Stop reading.　　　　(D) Stop talking.

女：不好意思，先生。你不能在機艙裡吸菸。

男：喔，我很抱歉。我會立刻把它熄滅。

女：謝謝你。

問題：這個女子要求男子做什麼？

選項：(A) 停止唱歌。　　(B) 停止抽菸。

　　　(C) 停止閱讀。　　(D) 停止說話。

提示：put...out 表示「熄滅……」。

---

45. W: Excuse me. I'm afraid you can't put your bag
in the aisle.

M: I'm sorry. Where should I put it?

W: You can put it under the seat in front of
you.

Q: What did the woman ask the man to do?

(A) Lay his bag in the aisle.

(B) Put down his tray table.

(C) Put his bag under the seat in front of him.

(D) Go back to his seat and fasten his seat belt.

女：不好意思。你恐怕不能將包包放在走道上。

男：很抱歉。我應該把它放在哪裡呢？

女：你可以將它放在你前面座位的下面。

問題：這個女子要求男子做什麼？

選項：(A) 把包包平放在走道上。

　　　(B) 放下摺疊桌。

　　　(C) 將包包置於前面的座位底下。

　　　(D) 回到自己的座位，並繫好安全帶。

此部分有 15 題，每題都有一張與該題目相對應的圖畫。請聽錄音機播出題目以及 A、B、C、D 四個英語敘述之後，選出與所看到的圖畫最相符的答案。每題只播出一遍。

1 _____

2 _____

3 _____

4 _____

5 _____

Allen Chen
No.890 Sanmin Rd.
Kaohsiung Taiwan

Airmail

Jennifer Li
P.O. Box 105
Sydney, NSW
Australia

6 _____

7 _____

8

9

10

11

12 _____

13 _____

14 _____

15 _____

Track #17

此部分有 15 題，每題請聽錄音機播出一個英語句子之後，從 A、B、C、D 四個回答或回應中，選出一個最適合者作答。每題只播出一遍。

_____ 16 (A) May I have your boarding pass?
　　　　 (B) May I see your baggage tag, please?
　　　　 (C) Follow the "Baggage Claim" sign.
　　　　 (D) No problem. Here you are.

_____ 17 (A) Sorry. We don't cash checks.
　　　　 (B) Sorry. We don't know the exchane rate.
　　　　 (C) Sure. How would you like it?
　　　　 (D) Sure. How much do you need?

_____ 18 (A) Sure. We don't collect any service charge.
　　　　 (B) Sure. Please fill out this form for me.
　　　　 (C) Yes. We only take US dollars here.

(D) Yes. We'll send someone over now.

19 (A) No. You can't smoke in your room.

(B) Sorry. Smoking isn't allowed here.

(C) Of course. I'll give you Room 1023.

(D) Yes. Just press "0" for front desk.

20 (A) Sure. We'll help you find it right now.

(B) Sure. I'll take care of this right away.

(C) Certainly. How would you like to pay?

(D) No problem. When will you be arriving?

21 (A) Yes. I can speak a little Japanese.

(B) Yes. You can take the MRT to get there.

(C) Yes. The price is not high and the food is good.

(D) Yes. There's one across the street from the hotel.

22 (A) Our business center will take care of it for you.

(B) I suggest the Italian restaurant on the 4th floor.

(C) Could you tell me your room number?

(D) Would you like to leave a message?

23 (A) Sure. I'll send someone to get it right now.

(B) Sure. You could do it in your own room.

(C) Do you need anything else?

(D) Could you take it back yourself?

24 (A) Sorry. I can't go with you.

(B) Sure. That's fine with me.

(C) I like Dutch food very much.

(D) I've never been to a Dutch restaurant.

25 (A) What's the problem, sir?

(B) Can you help me, sir?

(C) I'm sorry to hear that.

(D) Thank you very much.

26 (A) Certainly. Tomorrow will be fine.

(B) Of course. You can go by train.

(C) Yes. It should take at least two days.

(D) Yes. You can use express delivery.

27 (A) By surface mail, please.

(B) In the post office, please.

(C) In cash, please.

(D) By credit card, please.

28 (A) What did the sign say?

(B) Why do you ride a motorcycle?

(C) Sorry. I didn't notice you.

(D) Sorry. I didn't see the sign.

29 (A) I think your boss is a nice guy.

(B) I think I need your advice.

(C) I'm glad to hear that.

(D) I'm really sorry about that.

30 (A) That's nice. Going to the beach is

a great idea.

(B) I know. Some rest should do me good.

(C) I'm glad you'd like to go on a vacation.

(D) I hope your wife could recover soon.

此部分有 15 題，每題請聽錄音機播出一段對話及一個相關的問題，然後從 A、B、C、D 四個選項中挑出一個最適合的答案。每題只播出一遍。

_____ 31 (A) The woman is in Japan.
　　　　(B) The woman is traveling by herself.
　　　　(C) The woman has been to Japan before.
　　　　(D) The woman will meet two Japanese friends.

_____ 32 (A) The man is at the airport in Taipei.
　　　　(B) The man took a wrong baggage.
　　　　(C) The man couldn't find his baggage tag.
　　　　(D) The man's destination is San Francisco.

_____ 33 (A) At a gas station.
　　　　(B) At a bank.

(C) At a grocery store.

(D) At a restaurant.

34 (A) 10.　(B) 15.　(C) 20.　(D) 100.

35 (A) Get his passport.

(B) Pay his bill in cash.

(C) Buy some traveler's checks.

(D) Cash his traveler's checks.

36 (A) Housekeeping.　(B) Room Service.

(C) Front Desk.　(D) Laundry.

37 (A) US$5.　(B) US$10.

(C) US$15.　(D) US$20.

38 (A) 15.　(B) 20.　(C) 25.　(D) 50.

39 (A) Clothes.

(B) Books.

(C) Toys.

(D) All of the above.

40 (A) They ate too much.

(B) They stayed there too long.

(C) They were too polite.

(D) They were too noisy.

41 (A) He took pictures.

(B) He talked loudly.

(C) He touched the sculptures.

(D) He broke the warning sign.

42 (A) Call the police.

(B) Go to the hospital.

(C) Stay where he was.

(D) Stay away from the bank.

43 (A) A backache.   (B) A headache.

(C) A toothache.   (D) A sore throat.

44 (A) Drink a lot of water.

(B) Stop taking medicine.

(C) Take as much rest as possible.

(D) Take some vitamin and exercise.

45 (A) 30 minutes after each meal.

(B) One hour after each meal.

(C) 30 minutes before each meal.

(D) One hour before each meal.

1. What is the man saying to the woman?

(A) What's the purpose of your visit?

(B) May I see your passport?

(C) Welcome to the United States.

(D) I'll be staying at a youth hostel.

問題：這個男子正跟女子說什麼？

選項：(A) 請問你此行的目的是什麼？

　　　(B) 我可以看一下你的護照嗎？

　　　(C) 歡迎來到美國。

　　　(D) 我會住在青年旅社。

提示：圖中場景為機場的入境審查處
(Immigration)，故男子應正接受移民官的詢
問。選項(A)、(B)與(C)皆為移民官會與旅客說的
話，故選(D)。

2. What is the woman doing?

(A) Going through security.

(B) Asking for directions.

(C) Breaking large bills into smaller ones.

(D) Boarding an airplane.

問題：這個女子正在做什麼？

選項：(A) 通過安全檢查。

　　　(B) 問路。

　　　(C) 將大面額的鈔票換成較小的面額。

　　　(D) 登機。

3. What is the man saying to the woman?

(A) Here is your breakfast, ma'am.

(B) Everything looks fine. Thank you.

(C) Room service. May I help you?

(D) I'm sorry the TV isn't working.

問題：這個男子正跟女子說什麼？

選項：(A) 這是您的早餐，女士。

　　　(B) 每樣都看起來很好。謝謝你。

　　　(C) 客房服務。我能為您效勞嗎？

　　　(D) 我很抱歉電視壞掉了。

提示：選項(B)為服務生詢問房客餐點是否滿意，房客
　　　可能會回答的話。

4. What would the waitress say to the man?

(A) Here is the menu. I'll be back to take your order later.

(B) Thank you, sir. I'm glad you liked the chicken.

(C) I'm sorry. I'll bring you your chicken right

away.

(D) I'm sorry. I'll get you some coffee right now.

問題：這個女服務生會跟男子說什麼？

選項：(A) 這是菜單。稍後我會為您點餐。

(B) 謝謝您，先生。我很高興您喜歡這烤雞。

(C) 很抱歉。我會立刻送您的烤雞過來。

(D) 很抱歉。我現在就幫您送上咖啡。

---

5. Where will this letter be sent?

(A) Australia.   (B) Taiwan.

(C) No. 890.   (D) Airmail.

問題：這封信會被寄到哪裡？

選項：(A) 澳大利亞。   (B) 臺灣。

(C) 890 號。   (D) 航空郵寄。

---

6. Which is true?

(A) The woman is asking the man to light a cigarette for her.

(B) The woman is telling the man he can't smoke here.

(C) The man is handing over his cigarette to the woman.

(D) The man is moving to an area where he can smoke.

問題：何者屬實？

選項：(A) 女子正要男子幫她點菸。

　　　(B) 女子正告訴男子他不能在這抽菸。

　　　(C) 男子正將菸遞給女子。

　　　(D) 男子正要移到可以抽菸的區域。

提示：hand over 為「遞出」之意，hand 在此為動詞；light 在此亦為動詞，做「點燃」解。

- -

7. What happened to the boy?

　(A) He forgot to hand in his homework.

　(B) He was late for school.

　(C) He failed his test.

　(D) He got a high score.

問題：這個男孩怎麼了？

選項：(A) 他忘記繳交作業。

　　　(B) 他上學遲到了。

　　　(C) 他考試不及格。

　　　(D) 他得到高分。

提示：hand in 為「繳交」之意。

- -

8. How are the rescuers trying to save the woman?

　(A) Pulling her up with a lifebelt.

　(B) Rowing a boat over to save her.

(C) Swimming over to save her.

(D) Using a helicopter to get her out.

問題：救難隊員打算如何救起河裡的女子？

選項：(A) 以救生圈拉她上岸。

(B) 划一條船過去救她。

(C) 游泳過去救她。

(D) 開直昇機將她救起。

9. What is the woman saying to the man?

(A) I'd like to reserve a table for four tonight.

(B) The shower is leaking.

(C) How much is a double room?

(D) What time do you close tonight?

問題：這個女子正對男子說什麼？

選項：(A) 我想要預約今晚四人的位子。

(B) 蓮蓬頭一直在漏水。

(C) 一間雙人房多少錢？

(D) 你們今晚何時關門？

10. What is the man saying to the girls?

(A) You have to clean up the area before you leave.

(B) Fishing is not allowed here.

(C) Didn't you see the sign over there?

(D) Did you buy tickets at the entrance?

問題：這個男子正跟女孩們說什麼？

選項：(A) 你們得在離開前清理好這塊區域。

(B) 這裡禁止釣魚。

(C) 你們沒看到那邊的標誌嗎？

(D) 你們有在入口處買票嗎？

---

11. What does the man want to know?

(A) How much the bus fare is.

(B) Where he can catch a bus.

(C) Where the bus goes.

(D) When the next bus is.

問題：這個男子想知道什麼？

選項：(A) 巴士的票價是多少。

(B) 要到哪裡搭巴士。

(C) 巴士開往哪裡。

(D) 下一班巴士是什麼時候。

提示：圖中售票員的回答是金錢，故可推論男子在詢問價錢方面的事。

---

12. What is the woman saying?

(A) A coke will be fine.

(B) Check, please.

(C) Could you give me an extra napkin?

(D) Where is the washroom?

問題：這個女子在説什麼？

選項：(A) 一杯可樂就好。

　　　(B) 麻煩你，我要買單。

　　　(C) 你可以多給我一條餐巾嗎？

　　　(D) 洗手間在哪？

---

13. Which is true?

(A) A truck crashed into the river

(B) A building is on fire.

(C) There was a flood.

(D) An earthquake happened.

問題：何者屬實？

選項：(A) 卡車衝進了河裡。

　　　(B) 建築物著了火。

　　　(C) 這裡曾有水災。

　　　(D) 這裡發生了地震。

---

14. What do you see in the picture?

(A) The man is paying the check by cash.

(B) The man wants to order a cup of coffee.

(C) There is something wrong with the man's check.

(D) The cashier gave the man the wrong change.

問題：你在圖中看到了什麼？

選項：(A) 男子正用現金付帳。

(B) 男子想點一杯咖啡。

(C) 男子的帳單有問題。

(D) 收銀員給了男子錯誤的零錢。

提示：change 在此當名詞，表「零錢」；check 表「帳單」時為美式英語用法，英式英語則多用 bill。

---

15. What is the girl saying to the man?

(A) Thank you for all your help.

(B) Mind your own business.

(C) I don't like this dog.

(D) There's nothing you can do.

問題：這個女孩跟男子說什麼？

選項：(A) 謝謝你的幫忙。

(B) 管好你自己的事。

(C) 我不喜歡這隻狗。

(D) 你什麼也做不了。

第二部分　腳本與解析　 Track #17

16. Excuse me. I think my baggage is missing.

(A) May I have your boarding pass?

(B) May I see your baggage tag, please?

(C) Follow the "Baggage Claim" sign.

(D) No problem. Here you are.

問題：不好意思。我想我的行李不見了。

選項：(A) 能給我你的登機證嗎？

(B) 能讓我看你的行李牌嗎？

(C) 跟著「行李提領」的標誌。

(D) 沒問題。拿去吧。

---

17. Could you break a hundred for me?

(A) Sorry. We don't cash checks.

(B) Sorry. We don't know the exchange rate.

(C) Sure. How would you like it?

(D) Sure. How much do you need?

問題：你能幫我換這張百元鈔票嗎？

選項：(A) 抱歉。我們不兌現支票。

(B) 抱歉。我們不知道匯率是多少。

(C) 當然。您要怎麼換呢？

(D) 當然。您需要多少錢？

提示：break 在此為「兌開（大額鈔票）」的意思；
How would you like it? = How would
you like your money?，表示「你要將你的錢
換成什麼面額？」。

18. Could I exchange some Japanese Yen into NT dollars here?

   (A) Sure. We don't collect any service charge.

   (B) Sure. Please fill out this form for me.

   (C) Yes. We only take US dollars here.

   (D) Yes. We'll send someone over now.

   問題：我可以在這裡將一些日幣換成新臺幣嗎？

   選項：(A) 當然。我們不收取任何服務費。

   　　　(B) 當然。請幫我填寫這份表格。

   　　　(C) 可以。我們這裡只收美金。

   　　　(D) 可以。我們現在就派人過去。

----

19. Could you give me a room on a non-smoking floor?

   (A) No. You can't smoke in your room.

   (B) Sorry. Smoking isn't allowed here.

   (C) Of course. I'll give you Room 1023.

   (D) Yes. Just press "0" for front desk.

   問題：你可以給我一間在非吸菸樓層的房間嗎？

   選項：(A) 不行。您不能在房間裡抽菸。

   　　　(B) 抱歉。這裡禁止吸菸。

   　　　(C) 當然。我給您 1023 號房。

   　　　(D) 好的。撥「零」給櫃檯就好。

----

20. Could you get someone to take my baggage up to my room?

(A) Sure. We'll help you find it right now.

(B) Sure. I'll take care of this right away.

(C) Certainly. How would you like to pay?

(D) No problem. When will you be arriving?

問題：你能請人將行李拿上來我的房間嗎？

選項：(A) 當然。我們會馬上幫忙您找到它。

(B) 當然。我會馬上處理這件事情。

(C) 沒問題。您想要如何付帳？

(D) 沒問題。您什麼時候會到？

提示：take care of sth = deal with sth，表示「處理某事」之意。

....

21. Do you know any good Japanese restaurants near the hotel?

(A) Yes. I can speak a little Japanese.

(B) Yes. You can take the MRT to get there.

(C) Yes. The price is not high and the food is good.

(D) Yes. There's one across the street from the hotel.

問題：你知道飯店附近有任何不錯的日本餐廳嗎？

選項：(A) 是的。我能說一點日文。

(B) 是的。你可以搭乘大眾運輸去那裡。

(C) 是的。它的價格合理，且食物美味。

(D) 是的。有一間就在飯店的對面。

---

22. Hi, are there any messages for me?

(A) Our business center will take care of it for you.

(B) I suggest the Italian restaurant on the 4th floor.

(C) Could you tell me your room number?

(D) Would you like to leave a message?

問題：你好，有任何給我的留言嗎？

選項：(A) 我們的商務中心會幫您處理它。

　　　(B) 我建議四樓的義大利餐廳。

　　　(C) 您能告訴我您的房間號碼嗎？

　　　(D) 您想要留言嗎？

---

23. Hi, I'd like to have my suit ironed. Could you help me?

(A) Sure. I'll send someone to get it right now.

(B) Sure. You could do it in your own room.

(C) Do you need anything else?

(D) Could you take it back yourself?

問題：你好，我想要找人幫我燙西裝。你能幫我嗎？

選項：(A) 當然。我馬上派人去拿。

(B) 當然。您可以在自己的房間燙。

(C) 您還需要什麼嗎？

(D) 您能自己拿回去嗎？

---

24. Let's go Dutch.

(A) Sorry. I can't go with you.

(B) Sure. That's fine with me.

(C) I like Dutch food very much.

(D) I've never been to a Dutch restaurant.

問題：讓我們各付各的吧。

選項：(A) 抱歉。我不能跟你去。

(B) 好呀。我沒問題。

(C) 我很喜歡荷蘭的食物。

(D) 我從沒有去過荷蘭餐廳。

---

25. Excuse me. I think there's something wrong with the bill.

(A) What's the problem, sir?

(B) Can you help me, sir?

(C) I'm sorry to hear that.

(D) Thank you very much.

問題：不好意思。我想帳單有點問題。

選項：(A) 先生，有什麼問題嗎？

(B) 先生，您可以幫我嗎？

(C) 我很抱歉聽到那件事。

(D) 非常謝謝您。

---

26. Would it be possible for this package to reach
   Taichung tonight?

   (A) Certainly. Tomorrow will be fine.

   (B) Of course. You can go by train.

   (C) Yes. It should take at least two days.

   (D) Yes. You can use express delivery.

   問題：這個包裹有可能在今天晚上寄達臺中嗎？

   選項：(A) 當然。明天沒有問題。

   　　　(B) 當然。你可以搭火車去。

   　　　(C) 是的。那應該需要至少兩天。

   　　　(D) 是的。你可以用快遞寄送。

   提示：常用的寄信方式有：surface mail (平信)、
   　　　registered mail (掛號信)、express mail (快
   　　　遞) 和 airmail (航空信)。

---

27. How would you like to send this box?

   (A) By surface mail, please.

   (B) To the post office, please.

   (C) In cash, please.

   (D) By credit card, please.

問題：你想要怎麼寄送這個箱子？

選項：(A) 麻煩以平信寄送。

　　　(B) 麻煩到郵局。

　　　(C) 付現，謝謝。

　　　(D) 信用卡，謝謝。

---

28. You're not supposed to ride bicycles in here.

(A) What did the sign say?

(B) Why do you ride a motorcycle?

(C) Sorry. I didn't notice you.

(D) Sorry. I didn't see the sign.

問題：你不應該在這裡面騎腳踏車。

選項：(A) 告示牌上寫什麼？

　　　(B) 你為什麼要騎摩托車？

　　　(C) 抱歉。我沒有注意到你。

　　　(D) 抱歉。我沒有看見告示牌。

---

29. My boss fired me because of a difference of opinion.

(A) I think your boss is a nice guy.

(B) I think I need your advice.

(C) I'm glad to hear that.

(D) I'm really sorry about that.

問題：我的老闆因為意見分歧而解雇了我。

選項：(A) 我覺得你的老闆是位好人。

(B) 我想我需要你的建議。

(C) 我很高興聽見那個消息。

(D) 對那我真的感到很抱歉。

---

30. Maybe you should take a day off if you're not feeling well.

(A) That's nice. Going to the beach is a great idea.

(B) I know. Some rest should do me good.

(C) I'm glad you'd like to go on a vacation with me.

(D) I hope your wife could recover soon.

問題：如果你覺得不舒服，或許你應該請一天假。

選項：(A) 那很好。去海邊是個很棒的主意。

(B) 我知道。一些休息應該對我有好處。

(C) 我很高興你想要和我去渡假。

(D) 我希望你太太能早日康復。

提示：do sb good 表示「對某人有益處」。

第三部分 腳本與解析

Track #18

31. M: Are you traveling alone?

W: No. I'm traveling with two other friends.

M: I see. Have you ever been to Japan before?

W: No. This is my first time here.

Q: Which is true?

(A) The woman is in Japan.

(B) The woman is traveling by herself.

(C) The woman has been to Japan before.

(D) The woman will meet two Japanese friends.

男：你一個人旅行嗎？

女：不。我和另外兩個朋友一起。

男：我了解了。妳有來過日本嗎？

女：沒有。這是我第一次來這裡。

問題：何者屬實？

選項：(A) 這個女子在日本。

(B) 這個女子自己旅行。

(C) 這個女子曾經到過日本。

(D) 這個女子將和兩位日本友人見面。

---

32. M: Excuse me. My bag didn't come out with the other baggage.

W: What was your flight number?

M: CI680, flying from Taipei to San Francisco.

W: OK. I'll need your baggage tag. Let me check it for you.

Q: Which is true?

(A) The man is at the airport in Taipei.

(B) The man took a wrong baggage.

(C) The man couldn't find his baggage tag.

(D) The man's destination is San Francisco.

男：抱歉。我的包包沒有和其他行李一起出現。

女：您的班機號碼是什麼？

男：CI680，從臺北飛到舊金山。

女：好的。我需要您的行李牌。讓我幫您查查看。

問題：何者屬實？

選項：(A) 這個男子在臺北的機場。

　　　(B) 這個男子拿錯了行李。

　　　(C) 這個男子找不到他的行李牌。

　　　(D) 這個男子的目的地是舊金山。

---

33. M: May I help you?

W: Yes. I'd like to change some NT dollars into Japanese yen.

M: Sure. How much would you like to change?

W: I'd like to change 15,000 NT dollars.

Q: Where did this conversation take place?

(A) At a gas station.　　　(B) At a bank.

(C) At a grocery store.　　(D) At a restaurant.

男：我能為您效勞嗎？

女：是的。我想要將一些新臺幣換成日圓。

男：好的。您想要換多少錢？

女：我想要換新臺幣 15,000 元。

問題：這段對話在哪裡發生？

選項：(A) 在加油站。　　(B) 在銀行。

　　　(C) 在雜貨店。　　(D) 在餐廳。

提示：對話內容與外幣兌換有關，所以最有可能發生
在銀行，故選(B)。

---

34. W: Hi, could you break this NT$100-dollar bill
into small change for me?

M: Sure. How would you like it?

W: I'd like it all in tens.

M: No problem. Here you go.

Q: How many NT$10-dollar coins would the
woman get?

(A) 10.　　(B) 15.　　(C) 20.　　(D) 100.

女：你好，你可以幫我把這張百元鈔票換成零錢嗎？

男：當然。你要怎麼換呢？

女：如果可以的話，我想要都換成十元硬幣。

男：沒問題。拿去吧。

問題：這個女子會拿到多少個十元錢幣？

選項：(A) 10 個。　　　(B) 15 個。

　　　(C) 20 個。　　　(D) 100 個。

提示：因為這個女子想要將她的百元鈔票兌換為十
　　　元錢幣，故她會拿到十個十元錢幣。

---

35. M: I'd like to cash some traveler's checks,
　　　please.
　　W: OK, how much would you like to cash?
　　M: US$400.
　　W: I'll need your passport, and please sign these
　　　checks.
　　Q: What does the man want to do?
　　(A) Get his passport.
　　(B) Pay his bill in cash.
　　(C) Buy some traveler's checks.
　　(D) Cash his traveler's checks.
　　男：麻煩你，我想要兌現一些旅行支票。
　　女：好的，您要兌換多少現金呢？
　　男：四百美元。
　　女：我需要您的護照，並請在這些支票上簽名。
　　問題：這個男子想要做什麼？
　　選項：(A) 拿他的護照。
　　　　　(B) 以現金付帳。
　　　　　(C) 買一些旅行支票。
　　　　　(D) 兌現他的旅行支票。

36. M: Good morning. May I help you?

W: Yes. I'd like to have two American breakfasts sent up to Room 211.

M: No problem. We'll get them to you in about 20 minutes.

Q: Which department is the woman speaking to?

(A) Housekeeping.   (B) Room Service.

(C) Front Desk.   (D) Laundry.

男：早安。我能為您效勞嗎？

女：是的。我想要兩份美式早餐送到 211 房。

男：沒問題。我們大概在 20 分鐘內送去給您。

問題：這位女子在和哪個部門説話？

選項：(A) 房務部。   (B) 客房服務。

        (C) 櫃檯。   (D) 洗衣部。

提示：對話中的女子想要點餐，並希望能在房內用餐，由此可推知她打電話給客房服務。

- -

37. M: The bill is US$200. Shall we leave a tip?

W: Well, better check how much the service charge is.

M: Let me see. It's 15% of the bill.

W: OK. Let's leave another 10% for a tip.

Q: How much will they leave for a tip?

(A) US$5.　(B) US$10.　(C) US$15.　(D) US$20.

男：帳單是美金兩百元。我們應該留小費嗎？

女：嗯，最好看看服務費是多少。

男：讓我看看。是帳單的百分之十五。

女：好的。那我們另外留百分之十作為小費。

問題：他們將給多少小費？

選項：(A) 美金 5 元。　　(B) 美金 10 元。

　　　(C) 美金 15 元。　　(D) 美金 20 元。

提示：帳單總金額為美金兩百元，對話中男女決定留
　　　百分之十作為小費，故本題應選(A)。

---

38. M: Next, please.

W: Hi. I'd like to buy fifteen 25-cent stamps.

M: Sure. Here you are.

Q: How many stamps did the woman buy?

(A) 15.　　　(B) 20.　　　(C) 25.　　　(D) 50.

男：麻煩下一位。

女：你好。我想要買 15 張 25 分錢的郵票。

男：好的。拿去吧。

問題：這個女子買了幾張郵票？

選項：(A) 15 張。　　　　(B) 20 張。

　　　(C) 25 張。　　　　(D) 50 張。

---

39. M: Next, please.

W: Hi, I'd like to mail this box to Taiwan.

M: Sure. What's in the box?

W: Just some clothes, books, and toys. They are for my grandson.

Q: What is the woman mailing to her grandson?

(A) Clothes.　　　　　　(B) Books.

(C) Toys.　　　　　　　(D) All of the above.

男：麻煩下一位。

女：你好，我想要把這箱東西寄到臺灣。

男：好的。箱子裡面是什麼東西？

女：就一些衣服、書籍和玩具。它們是要給我孫子的。

問題：這個女子寄什麼東西給她的孫子？

選項：(A) 衣服。　　　　(B) 書籍。

　　　(C) 玩具。　　　　(D) 以上皆是。

- -

40. M: Excuse me, ma'am. Could you please ask your children to stop running around and be quiet? The behavior is not allowed here in our café.

W: Oh, I'm so sorry. I'm stopping them now.

M: Thank you.

Q: What did the woman's children do wrong?

(A) They ate too much.

(B) They stayed there too long.

(C) They were too polite.

(D) They were too noisy.

男：不好意思，太太。能請你告訴你的小孩不要跑來跑去，並且安靜一點嗎？在我們的咖啡館裡是不允許這些行為的。

女：喔，我很抱歉。我這就制止他們。

男：謝謝你。

問題：這個女子的小孩做錯了什麼？

選項：(A) 他們吃太多東西。

　　　(B) 他們待在那裡太久。

　　　(C) 他們太有禮貌了。

　　　(D) 他們太吵了。

---

41. W: Excuse me, sir. You're not supposed to touch these sculptures.

M: Oh, I'm very sorry. They are so beautiful!

W: That's why we put a warning sign at the entrance. If everyone touches them, they might be damaged easily.

M: Yes. You're right. I won't do it again.

Q: What did the man do wrong?

(A) He took pictures.

(B) He talked loudly.

(C) He touched the sculptures.

(D) He broke the warning sign.

女：不好意思，先生。你不該觸碰這些雕像。

男：喔，我很抱歉。它們太美了！

女：這就是我們在門口放置警示牌的原因。如果每個人都觸碰它們，它們可能很容易就毀損了。

男：是的。你說得沒錯。我不會再犯了。

問題：這個男子做錯了什麼？

選項：(A) 他拍了照。

(B) 他大聲說話。

(C) 他觸碰了雕像。

(D) 他破壞了警示牌。

---

42. M: Hello, I heard several gunshots coming from inside the bank.

W: Where are you?

M: Outside the East-west Bank on Center Street.

W: OK. The police will be there right away. For your own safety, don't go any closer to the bank.

Q: What did the woman tell the man to do?

(A) Call the police.

(B) Go to the hospital.

(C) Stay where he was.

(D) Stay away from the bank.

男：喂，我聽到幾聲槍響從銀行裡傳出來。

女：你在哪裡？

男：在中央街上的東西銀行外面。

女：好的。警察馬上就會過去。為了你自身安全，不要再靠近銀行。

問題：這個女子要男子做什麼？

選項：(A) 打電話報警。　(B) 去醫院。
　　　(C) 待在原地。　　(D) 遠離銀行。

---

43. M: I don't feel good, doc.

W: What's wrong?

M: My throat hurts when I talk.

W: Let me see. Hmm. I'll give you some medicine. Drinking some warm salt water will also help.

Q: What problem did the man have?

(A) A backache. 　　　　(B) A headache.

(C) A toothache. 　　　(D) A sore throat.

男：我覺得不太舒服，醫生。

女：怎麼了？

男：我說話時喉嚨會痛。

女：讓我看看。嗯。我會開一些藥給你。喝一些溫的鹽水也有幫助。

問題：這個男子有什麼問題？

選項：(A) 背痛。　　　　(B) 頭痛。

　　　(C) 牙痛。　　　　(D) 喉嚨痛。

---

44. W: Doctor, I still feel dizzy when I stand up.

M: Did you take the medicine I gave you?

W: Yes. I've been drinking a lot of water, too.

M: Well, stay in bed. You need more rest.

Q: What did the man advise the woman to do?

(A) Drink a lot of water.

(B) Stop taking medicine.

(C) Take as much rest as possible.

(D) Take some vitamin and exercise.

女：醫生，我站起來時還是會頭暈。

男：你有服用我開給你的藥嗎？

女：有。我也一直喝很多水。

男：嗯，待在床上。你需要更多休息。

問題：這個男子建議女子什麼？

選項：(A) 喝很多水。

　　　(B) 停止服藥。

　　　(C) 休息越多越好。

　　　(D) 服用一些維他命和運動。

---

45. W: Could you be more specific about when I

should take the pills?

M: Yes. Take them half an hour after each meal.

W: Thanks.

M: You're welcome.

Q: When should the woman take her pills?

(A) 30 minutes after each meal.

(B) One hour after each meal.

(C) 30 minutes before each meal.

(D) One hour before each meal.

女：你可以更明確地告訴我什麼時候該服藥嗎？

男：好的。每餐飯後半小時服用它們。

女：謝謝。

男：不客氣。

問題：這個女子什麼時候該服用她的藥？

選項：(A) 每餐飯後三十分鐘。

(B) 每餐飯後一小時。

(C) 每餐飯前三十分鐘。

(D) 每餐飯前一小時。

全民英檢
聽力測驗 SO EASY

中級篇

增強聽力 SO EASY

- 內含八回聽力模擬試題，增加實戰經驗。
- 提供三種聽力型態的範例分析，精闢解說考試重心。
- 由專業外籍老師錄製精采聽力內容MP3，完全模擬測驗題目的間隔與速度，讓您提高應試的熟悉度。

Vocabulary 7000 隨身讀

隨時滿足您讀的渴望。

- 口袋型設計易帶易讀,分秒必爭學習最有效率。
- 廣納7000個必考單字,依據使用頻率排列,分級學習最科學。
- 增補重要同反義字與常見片語,助您舉一反三、觸類旁通。